Junk Man

a novella

Erec Stebbins

New York, NY, USA

"Only one thing is impossible for God: To find any sense in any copyright law on the planet." - Mark Twain

This book is a work of fiction. Any references to historical events, real people, or real locales are used fictitiously. Other names, characters, places, and incidents are the product of the author's imagination, and any resemblance to actual events or locales or persons, living or dead, is entirely coincidental.

Published 2013 by Twice Pi Press
Inquiries should be addressed to
TwicePiPress@gmail.com

TWICE PI PRESS

Paperback
ISBN-10: 0615763839
ISBN-13: 978-06157638-3-5

Hardback
ISBN-10: 098900046X
ISBN-13: 978-0-9890004-6-8

For Ria

Summoner of Good Monsters

Preface

This is an old story, both in its setting and in the chronology of my life. It was my first piece of prose beyond a short story. It is ridiculously ambitious, written from the eyes of American society's most ignorant and often most wise, impoverished and abused, in a facsimile of various Southern dialects, about topics the young man I once was might ought to have postponed taking on as subjects.

But like most "real" stories that come from within, the narrative had a will of its own. I had no plans to write *Junk Man* – it had plans for me. My old friend Insomnia visited in Greece while seeing family there, and suddenly in the middle of the night my protagonists began speaking in my mind. Taking forms. The story was fleshed out roughly by morning. Their voices were strong, real, and would not be denied. So, I wrote them as best as I could.

The narrative also commandeered my memories, and the tales of others I have witnessed. *Their* stories were ripped out of time and context, thrown into an Acme Story Blender 5000 along with completely fictional elements, and the "pulse crush" button depressed until what remained was a soup of tragedy with the forensics of a Jackson Pollock painting.

In that sense, *Junk Man* is both the least accurate and the *truest* story I've ever written: The least accurate for all the blending, mixing, matching, and selective use of human woe; the truest because, in my subjective sense of truth, the essence of the pain and human frailty in those deconstructed and reformed narratives remains intact.

The attempts to recreate the impressions of various regional dialects should be taken in the spirit intended: not as an academically accurate transliteration (for which the written English language is unsuitable), nor as an effort to quickly and grotesquely stereotype the speakers of these musical accents, but as an honest endeavor to remember and capture the spirit floating above the people who learn the rhythms and intonations of any language. For me there would have been something missing in the story had it been rendered in "standard English" (whatever that is in whatever age), however imperfect my attempts here.

For all of our waste and brokenness, for all our clumsiness in life and matters of the heart, there has always been a mythology of redemption. Of resurrection. Of renewal.

In that spirit, I give you *Junk Man*.

Erec Stebbins

January 7, 2013, NYC

Every man is a divinity in disguise, a god playing the fool. It seems as if heaven had sent its insane angels into our world as to an asylum, and here they will break out into their native music and utter at intervals the words they have heard in heaven; then the mad fit returns, and they mope and wallow like dogs.

-Ralph Waldo Emerson, "Essays"

1

It never would'a come out if I weren't made to go to that no good couns'lin'. I never told no secret before, leastways not one so impor'ant. I told a friend once, but he ain't the type that'll gossip 'bout no secret, I can promise you. Yeah, but I let it slip. You might too, if'n they made you sit a whole dang hour in that couns'lin', lis'nin' to 'em size you up who ain't knowed no first thing 'bout you. You might do worse. But that's where it all started, anyhow.

First day I went, he said somethin' like, "Hi there, son. My name's Mr. Robertson, but most of the children like to call me Uncle John."

Well, he was a nice 'nuff man and all that I s'ppose, but he weren't my uncle. I ain't got no Uncle

John. I've got an Uncle Mike and an Uncle Billy, but since Ma and Pa split up I don't see 'em too much no more. I see my Uncle Dave, but he lives outside in the country, up along the Trail, like we used to, but it's too far to go so much nowadays.

"Hi there, Sir." was what I said.

"We pride ourselves at the Johnson School in meeting the needs of all our students. And for special kids like you, Josh, whose Mom and Dad have divorced, and who seem, well, challenged in other aspects of our academic enterprise, we like to make sure that you feel comfortable and at home in our school."

I never liked that word, divorced. It don't mean nothin'. I mean, split up sounds right, 'cause my Ma and Pa are like a piece of wood that you took hard to your knee. And I didn't much care for the way he was sayin' *challenged*. But Mr. Robertson talked in a big way, and there weren't much to do but wait 'til he finished. So, that's what I did. Like always, I started thinkin' on other things.

Me and the others, the ones like me whose folks split up, or some others who was always gettin' in trouble, had to go once a week for a whole hour, sometimes even more, and talk to him. Seems like it was somethin' big lots'a folk thought was special, or made 'em and the school special, anyways. Can't say that it seems all that special to me, 'less you mean in the way that there ain't nothin' else like it, which for some things, you might say, ain't so bad.

Most of the time he was askin' me lots of questions and always lookin' real int'rested, like when Aunt Jane comes by and talks at Ma 'bout all that happened bad to her the last week, and Ma smiles real pretty. I never figured why he was so keen on knowin' 'bout my dreams and if I thought 'bout Pa and all other kinda things. To tell you right up, I never think much on it. Me and my brother, Tom, we was always doin' stuff, like when we used to fight wars in the old woods, or like now watchin' boats down by the dock. Ain't no point in thinkin' on all that other stuff. But Mr. Robertson never let up, and he was always makin' me talk 'bout it. That's another reason why I didn't much like talkin' to him.

No one I knowed did, anyways. There was some of us at the school not from 'round here, and most'a those was from the country like me. Well, it weren't easy fittin' in with all our accents and funny dress and all. My Ma said I'm right losin' my accent and soundin' like the city folk, but I reckon I'm more like a mixed dog, takin' some'a here, some'a there from everythin' and not really endin' up bein' nothin', really. Well, it didn't help none to fittin' in that I hadda go see Mr. Robertson ev'ry week, that I can tell you. But I don't care, 'cause there ain't no point in cryin' over what someone else did to you.

I mean, it ain't like I hate school or nothin'. Oftentimes there's fun or friends or at least somethin' int'restin'. But more often'an not, somethin's bound to rise up, pretty much ev'ry day really, that just plain ruins any good thing you had goin' before. And I don't know 'bout you, but with me, it seems like 'em bad things got a way of stickin' with me longer than any good things. It's a shame, really, but that's how it is, even if I wish it was diff'rent. Most days all I got left is like some bad taste you got from burnt food. Happens all the time, really.

Like the time I was walkin' home, 'bout to leave the school, out the back movin' past the dumpsters behind the lunchroom, when all a sudden these boys start haulin' tomaters at me from the trash. Now, I weren't askin' for no trouble, and I don't really go in for fightin' no one, but this just set me off. I mean, I didn't do 'em no harm, so why they gotta go and do that and ruin my clothes so that Ma'll light into me when I get home? So, I picked up them that they throwed and pelted 'em good. I got a right good arm, a nat'ral my Pa used to say, or helluva good shot, which is what it is. Well, just when I was givin' it back to 'em, a door opens and some ol' teacher sees me throwin' tomaters and 'em two cryin' 'bout it.

So, I get drug off by her up to some other teacher I never met, blamed for it all. He was some coach or somethin', and had a shiny bald head, and it was like he was ironed all over. He showed me a wood paddle he kept on his desk, I s'ppose, all the time. It had names signed all over it. He told me that those he whupped wrote their name on it. But he didn't ask me to write mine, though he whupped me good, five times he hit me so that I couldn't see for cryin'. The worst part was I had to go back out the school lookin' like such a sissy, and I was lucky most all the kids was home already. But I never would'a signed it, even if he'd a hit me fifty times. Just thinkin' 'bout all 'em names on it turns my stomach, like they was dead and their names wrote down like they did for those killed soldiers from 'Nam on that black wall up north.

Another bad day was when I called that girl fat. Don't get me wrong, I don't go around much sayin' hurtful things to people, even if it's true, which this was, as she was the danged fattest person I ever saw. And she weren't shy like some other fat people. She weren't even nice. It was like she was mad at ev'ryone for God makin' her so fat like that, and she was always loud and pushin' folk around. Well, we were all waitin' in line for the bus, me and some friends and others, when she comes cuttin' right in front, pushin' me back, and not even makin' up some lie or sayin' she was sorry. And it ain't easy havin' some girl push you 'round in front other boys, even if she was a whole lot bigger'an you are.

Well, I s'ppose I lost my religion, and just said somethin' 'bout her bein' fat and rude and whatnot. To tell you the truth, I don't recall much'a that day, 'cause after I said it, she spun 'round and clocked me, whipped her hand 'cross my face so hard I had trouble seein' straight. I mean, 'less you been hit hard in the head, which I been, mostly by Pa after I was actin' up, it's hard to tell you what it's like. Maybe like your brain was knocked outside your head but your eyes stayed there, but your ears went with your brain, and you don't know where ev'rythin' else went. Anyway, I didn't cry that time. Not 'cause some boys were there, which, you know, would'a been smart. But ev'rythin' was rattlin' 'round so much I don't think I really felt much of anythin'. I didn't even know I was bleedin' 'til I got home. Got a nice scar from it too, shaped like a diamond, right on my left cheek. But if anyone asks, I don't say nothin' 'bout that story, and no one there, not my friends or that fat girl, ever said nothin' to me 'bout it neither.

And with all 'em classes and work and all of it so borin', and with all the troubles with people and populars and whatnot, you have to find ways to make somethin' int'restin' at school, even if it's just pushin' chairs 'round in that AV room. That's my own trick, when ev'rybody's watchin' films. I almost never been catched doin' it, even if folks s'pect me, now. It ain't hard, really, just needs patience, like most things, I reckon. Not that you really care, but here's what you do. After a few minutes watchin' a movie, people start gettin' into it and a yella jacket could fly right on their arm and they wouldn't know 'til it was too late. So, they don't notice too much of nothin', and that's good for doin' some fun things.

My thing with chairs don't hurt no one, and I reckon it's pretty dumb, really. But I always think it's funny. So, you put your feet at the back legs 'em chairs. It only works with the flat metal feet on the short carpet like in the AV room. So, you push real slow for a long time. That's it, really. A little and a little more. Soon, all the little pushes add up to a long way, and all of a sudden they snap out of it and they see they're in the next county! Well, anyway, makes me laugh.

To get to what I was fixin' to tell you, one day I was stuck with that Mr. Robertson, and he was showin' me these pit'chers, if you was the kind that'd call 'em that. Whoever made 'em can't draw worth a God damn, if you'll excuse my French. They was so bad he asked me what I thought was on 'em! Well, at first I said nothin' but a lot of ink, mainly 'cause I was tired of all his askin', but that didn't stop ol' Mr. Robertson, no Sir. He kept tellin' me to look harder. I thought maybe my eyes was tired. They get like that when I look at the board too long. Teacher says I need glasses but Ma says no, and anyway, I ain't wearin' no sissy glasses just so as I can read better. So, I looked harder, but I still saw nothin' but that ink. So, I thought I'd better make up somethin', else I'd never get outta that room. I tried to think on somethin' that'd fool him, and it was then that I recalled 'bout the Junk Man.

I ain't told no one else 'bout him before but my friend Toby, who saw him once. You see, right as I was lookin' at that ink, I thought on somethin' I seen in the museum. The Junk Man, he had a real nice museum behind his house. Well, it weren't much a house. A shack my Ma would'a called it. And it weren't much a museum, least not like those we seen on field trips. It was made a some old throw'way sheet the Junk Man found somewheres. He was always findin' stuff and makin' somethin' with it. So, it weren't so much a buildin' even. But it was what was *inside* that made it real nice, but I'll tell you 'bout that later. So, there was this rose in the museum, and if you maybe were to go and paint it black and squash it all up and let it get all dried out, and looked at it just the right way, I bet it could'a looked somethin' like that ink he was a-holdin' up.

So, I said, "It looks like the Alter Rose," and he seemed real s'prised.

"What's that, Josh?"

"It's in the Junk Man's museum," I said.

"Who's the junk man, Josh?"

And that's how I done it. I never did mean to tell no one and I'm awful sorry I did, but you can't change what's been done. That's what my Pa used to say: *What's done's, done.* Like when he chopped 'em chicken's heads off, pow! They'd go runnin' all 'round the backyard of the old house. We left the old house, and I think that was the worse of all, since I liked it so much. But you can't put the heads back on 'em chickens. So, I'm sorry I told 'bout the Junk Man, but what's done's, done.

Well, now I'd really done it, and there was so many questions I can't recall 'em no more. But it was one thing in the end. He wanted to hear the story 'bout the Junk Man. That's what I wanted to tell you in the first place, now that it don't matter no more 'cause he's gone.

Should be gone, anyway. But I always feel like that he's right near me, that if I turn 'round real fast, he'd be there givin' me that wink and smile with all 'em missin' teeth and laughin' real hard at somethin' I was doin'.

But I ain't never seen him no more after they took him away.

2

I met the Junk Man when I was sneakin' in the Trash Yard. That's what we call it, us kids livin' 'round it. It's got some other name the city gives it, but that ol' sign's rusted and half-falled apart so as you can't read it no more. I s'ppose it's junk, too, now. But it's a great place to do all kinda things and find all kinda stuff.

Like bottle caps. My brother and me was always goin' 'round and findin' bottle caps. We was collectin' 'em, you see. We must've had a thousand bottle caps in diff'rent shoe boxes and such. I don't rightly know what we was figurin' on doin' with 'em all. Likely as not nothin', like ev'rythin' else we started and never finished. I think the main fun was findin' 'em and seein' the collection keep gettin' bigger all the time. We found all kinda other things too. Like cowboy belts. I always liked those, 'specially those with 'em giant belt buckles with horns or horses and whatnot. People always throwin' stuff out. All kinda diff'rent things. I found some old paintin's too, good as some you might see on folk's walls.

A bunch of the boys was always lookin' for 'em magazines with all 'em nekked girls. Sometimes I liked lookin' at 'em too, to tell you the truth. Specially those with showin' their boobs and all. I mean, you ain't seen girls like that too much, their boobs bein' so big 'bout to bust out the page but the girls not bein' fat nowhere else or nothin'. I like those too that had nice faces, like they was friendly and nice and all. But some have other looks which ain't so nice. Those weren't my fav'rits.

Anyways, lots of us went there. My brother Tom 'bout killed me there once. For real. They had some old big dumpsters near the fences, and sometimes we was lookin' inside 'em for things. Well, I was walkin' behind one this day and pow! Right on the top'a my head my brother opens one of 'em big metal doors that swings on over and down to the ground. 'Cept this one hit my head first, hit me so hard it knocked me so as I was kneelin' like a preacher. When I was tryin' to get up I touched my head and saw all this red blood all over my hand. Soon it was runnin' all down my face like a river so I couldn't see for all the blood. I ran home screamin' and my Ma took me to the 'mergency room and I got seven stitches in my head. I lied to her and said I fell down on some rocks.

And that weren't the only time I got bloody there, in the Trash Yard. Once, we was havin' a rock fight with these other boys when one of 'em hit me right in the nose with a rock. I had to go home for that, too. I told Ma that it was a rock fight, but I didn't say nothin' 'bout whcrc. She said I was a dang fool. I s'ppose she was right.

So, you see, we never told our folks, as they would'a killed us right on the spot for goin' there. It was easy to get in, too. Old Man Morris, he's the guard and can't hear so good no more, never catches us, and the fence ain't been fixed I suspect in forever. So there's good sized holes for a kid like me to squeeze in. That's the tricky part, 'cause you don't want to tear your shirt or pants. There's always trouble at home for tearin' stuff.

And I got real good at gettin' in. Oftentimes, I'd go with Toby and some other boys, sometimes just myself. I even went once with this girl from the high school, but that was kinda confusin'. I reckon now she was kinda pullin' one on me, 'cause I didn't know so much. I ain't never had much to do with girls, even if I was thirteen. I mean, Toby and me, we saw some parts of 'em films, but it never made much sense to me all that pushin' and gruntin'. Well, this girl she tells me she knows all 'bout that, and how I should learn to be a man. So, I followed her and she went to the Trash Yard and found a place.

So, there was just an old mattress throwed out and junk all 'round hidin' it, but she tells me to pull down my shorts. Now, openin' ev'rythin' up down there just ain't for anywhere, anytime. Or anyone, 'least of all not some girl I just met who was standin' out in the Trash Yard with me.

I ain't never got all nekked like that for no one, 'cept my folks and the doctor. Like that time when I got that tick on my dick. Yeah, I ain't foolin' you. You'd wonder how of all the places a boy'd get a danged tick how it'd find its way there. I mean, Tom, my cousins, heck, even Pa had ticks on all kinda places like arms and legs. Their neck. That was 'bout once a month goin' through all the woods up along the trails and such. Ever'body got 'em. But I never heard nobody else ever got one on their privates.

I found it peein' after we got back. I was aimin' and my fingers felt somethin' big and round, hard on the other side of my dick. I flipped it around and there was a fat old, black tick right in the middle. 'Course at first I wasn't gonna tell no one and was fixin' to take it off myself, but if you lived in these parts and ev'ryone's gettin' 'em ticks, shoot, you know things can go right bad if you don't take 'em off right. You want trouble down there? Well, I didn't.

So, I had to go and get myself all embarrassed tellin' my folks that I had a tick on my dick. My brother 'bout thought it was the funniest thing he ever did hear. I think Pa was tryin' to hold it all in, too, and maybe didn't half b'lieve me 'til he saw it. So, there I was sittin' on that leather chair in front of the winda, you know, to have good lightin', and my pants was down and my privates wavin' to the world while ev'ryone in my house was standin' 'round me like those docs on TV, Pa with a match and some pliers.

You know how you get ticks out, right? You bring somethin' hot close to 'em. Not too hot, 'cause you might kill 'em and then they stick and rot inside and that's bad. Or they feel it and pull out too fast. You gotta make 'em just a little hot, and then they come out slow until you can pull 'em. All that's fine with fire and plicrs and people 'round if'n it's your leg. But when it's your dick in front of the winda there's just somethin' terrible wrong with the world.

Anyway, so I got this scar there now, a round one from that tick on my dick. But I didn't think of that then, with that girl. That tick was far outta my mind. When she wanted me to pull down my shorts, it was a diff'rent feelin', and I was kinda scared. I was gonna leave, but she was sayin' how I was just a little boy and not a man. Well, that weren't gonna happen, as all 'em boys seen us go and were sayin' how I was gonna score and all. So, I did drop 'em shorts, and she took off her shirt and she didn't have no bra underneath. I ain't never seen a girl all nekked so close, and I felt real funny. Then, she startin' touchin' me all over, and I bet you can guess the rest.

Least, I hope you can, as some things just too hard to tell all 'bout to anyone. So, I'm sure you know how that all goes. It was sure new to me. I ain't never knowed how some other person could make you feel and do whatever they wanted just by touchin' you, like it don't matter what you think you want or try to do or nothin', but she had me doin' whatever so'ans I couldn't stop her at all. Like your own body weren't yours no more. You know what I mean.

Anyways, after it was over, she was laughin' real hard and said that I was a real man. It was all so quick and easy, becomin' a man, and I felt all empty like when you ain't eaten for all day, and kinda scared, but it shut 'em boys up after that, let me tell you. I never knowed why she did that. Toby said she did that with lots of boys, and that she took drugs at the high school. Sometimes, I'd look for her, I don't know why, but after that year she didn't come 'round no more. Nobody could say where she went.

Which is just as good, I s'ppose, 'cause to tell you the truth, I still ain't sure 'bout all that bein' a man stuff. I mean, even if we was doin' it back there in the Trash Yard like I said, which we was, I ain't tellin' no tall one, afterwards if I looked at the older boys, you know, high school boys, I think I ain't there yet, or somethin'. Somethin's missin', I mean, but I don't know what. Maybe that girl messed it up, even if she sure seemed to know what she was doin'. Maybe I was s'pposed to do somethin' else, maybe that's why she were laughin' at the end of it.

To tell you the truth, I don't know nothin' 'bout it. Yeah, mor'in likely it was my fault, like too many things, I s'ppose. I don't know, maybe all that talk's just bull, 'bout scorin' makin' you a man and all. Maybe there's gotta be somethin' else you gotta do to make it happen. I s'ppose that's my feelin'. All scorin' did was feel great for a minute and then lousy for weeks, but had me still sorta wishin' I'd get to do it again. Hard to figure. But it's right curious - I was never feelin' so lonely 'til I got together with that girl. That one from the Trash Yard that I never saw no more.

Well, if you're gonna hear 'bout the Junk Man, I reckon you can hear it all, leastways 'bout that tick and how that girl pulled one on me. I s'ppose sometimes you need to tell things to someone you ain't ever knowed, 'cause your friends after a while know too much 'bout you, like they was yourself. And you never can go trustin' your own advices. I mean, I don't know exactly why I'm tellin' you 'bout the Junk Man. Just sorta had to, 'cause for me knowin' him was somethin' changin' my life, and you seemed int'rested enough. Well, least so far.

Anyway, it was spring and I was lookin' 'round the Trash Yard when I saw the strangest site you ever did see. Bendin' over a big heap was a man all wrapped up in a coat, but it was close to summer. He had one of those beards like 'em homeless men in the park, and it was long and black with gray runnin' like spilled silver down through it. He must've been old, 'cause he was real bent over, even when he was just standin' still, and his hands were all full'a veins like thin ol' folks have, bulgin' out like some man's arm pumpin' iron down at the gym by the dock, 'cept without all 'em muscles.

And he was a leper, too. I knowed this first minute I saw him pickin' through all that trash. That's 'cause the boys at school, when they made us go to the library, we was always lookin' through books for better pit'chers. Could'a been them nekkid girls outta Africa or some kinda nasty sickness that made you wanna hand back your lunch. That's where I saw all 'em leper pit'chers, what with all 'em bumps 'cross their faces and scars and fingers missin' and such. That's what I was seein' 'cross the way there a-huntin' in that garbage. Ugly as sin and made your skin crawl for bein' afeared it was catchin', which bein' a leper sure was, let me tell you. I ain't never heard'a no one seein' a leper, nowadays. What I heard tell was they put 'em all down Louisiana and can cure 'em all at the hospitals. So, I guess the Junk Man ain't never got to no hospital else he'd'a been cured up'a that leper sickness.

My Ma would'a whupped me just for bein' there lookin' at him, 'cause she tells me never to hang 'round with no strangers 'cause things might be wrong with 'em. And bein' a leper likely was near the top'a her list if'n she'd ever thought I might'a seen one.

Likely the only worser thing would'a been if'n he was colored. Well, we used to use other words for 'em where I used to live, up in the mountains, before we moved here to the city. But I learned we ain't s'pposed to use 'em words here. You gotta say colored or black, even if most of 'em are brown. And you know, white folks ain't really white, neither. White folks can be kinda pink, or yellow, or in the summer brown, sometimes browner than the coloreds. Then, you got them Injuns, they call 'em Red Man, even if they ain't at all red. Or the Chinamen they callin' yella, and they seem 'bout as yella as white folks is white. Hell, up near the Trail, we heard stories 'bout *blue* people, even. That's the God's honest truth. Folks the color blue. Pa said he knowed a family up the Trail a ways that had a boy who was the bluest damn person he ever saw. So, I don't see what all this fuss is 'bout colors when it don't mean no damn thing. But us country kids got a bad word out on us 'bout it all.

I s'ppose you think that way, too, maybe that I'm some country fool who hates all 'em black folk. What they callin' prej'diced here. I think my Ma and Pa is prej'diced. Pa said before the Civil War, ev'ryone had his place, meanin' the whites and blacks. He had some old trunk in the attic with Confed'rate money, funny lookin' money like you ain't never seen, I bet. He said his Pa told him to save it 'cause the South would rise again. That meant fightin' another war, I reckon. So that 'em damn Yankees wouldn't tell the blacks and whites how to live. Damn Yankees was what he called the ones from the North that came down and killed and ruined ev'rything. "Ah was twelve years old before Ah knowed damn Yankee was two words," Pa used to say, which didn't make no sense, as it's clear like day they's two words. But there weren't gonna be no arguin' that with him.

But I don't see any risin' up again happenin'. All that Confed'rate money's gonna stay up there, 'long with all 'em guns he don't shoot and the riggin' for the 'shine. That's moonshine, which my gran'pa made a long time ago. Pa likes talkin' 'bout that, too, how they didn't care none 'bout the law and sold it. He said there was bottles and bottles in the basement when he was a young'un like me, and gran'pa made him whistle when he'd send him down to fetch it, 'less he'd get to a-drinkin' some the way up. That's another thing that never made no sense to me. I tried that 'shine once, and let me tell you, you ain't gotta ask me to whistle or whatnot – I ain't drinkin' that no more 'less'n I get a notion to burn a hole in my belly.

Anyways, Pa might be some prej'diced , but he weren't all prej'diced, 'cause he said he thought 'em colored folks were cute when they was little, but not when they growed up. So, Pa liked 'em sometimes, leastways. I don't think Ma liked 'em noways. She was always scared of 'em, especially the boys. She said no white woman was safe alone with 'em, and after her and Pa split up, when we moved down here, it's like she weren't never goin' out alone at night. She even got herself a gun that she keeps next to her bed, which don't make no sense as she ain't got no heart on usin' it. But I s'ppose havin' it there makes her thinkin' like she can.

Speakin' for myself, I don't hold nothin' against no one 'less he done wronged me. But the black kids, well, they hate the white kids and let you know it good. And the white kids hate 'em right back. It's all divided up at the school, like a divorce or worse really, and no one's friends with the other, and they're mean like wild pigs if they catch you alone.

I know, 'cause for one it happened to me. I was comin' in by way of the gym door one day, which I never did before or ever again after that day, 'cause in that hall is where the blacks get together. Seein' me comin', 'cause I ain't so big as you can see or nothin', a small white boy all alone 'bout set 'em right off like a bunch'a dogs on the hunt. First, they was sayin' things and laughin' at my cloths, which bein' from the country was right diff'rent from city stuff, but it still don't feel so good when they laughin' at you. Then, things got worse fast, just as I was gettin' out to the main hall some at the end stepped in the middle and made it so I had to push 'em out the way to get by. I was gettin' scared then, let me tell you, 'cause they was really gettin' mean, and lookin' mad and sayin' awful things. I just panicked, I s'ppose, and put my head down and ran through and busted out to the hall and was safe. I don't know what they was aimin' to do to me. So, it's tough for white folks if they don't stick together, like most do. But white folks is just as bad as 'em coloreds linin' the hall if they catch some poor black kid alone. I know that, too, 'cause I seen it, and he didn't get away like I did, and 'em white boys just beat him to the dirt, they did, right outside the school. And no one did nothin'.

It all makes me tired really, and I ain't got much use for it, but that's how it is, and I reckon, with all that you're bound to have to hate someone before it's all done.

Anyway, so him bein' a leper, the Junk Man, maybe even worse than a colored, that was in my head that day I first saw him, with his long coat and all. And he was dirty, too. Dirty, I s'ppose from touchin' all the trash, all the day. The hard part, you might guess, 'bout the Trash Yard, was the smell. I mean there was all sorta junk and rotten things from all of creation piled up. And there he was, bendin' over, stickin' his scarred-up hands deep into it all, drippin' sometimes, tossin' it around. His shoes, if you felt like callin' 'em shoes what with all the holes and tears, had mud and dust and who knows what stuck to 'em. Yeah, he stunk, like the Trash Yard, and flies followed him around. You might wonder why some kid like me would stay long to look at such.

But it was funny, you know? He didn't seem so dirty when he looked at you and you saw his eyes. Well, you hadda stop starin' at his face, all 'em bumps and holes and stuff, which weren't so easy a thing to do, let me say. You ever stood close up to some dirt-ugly person? I ain't never seen no one so ugly. But if'n you could get past all that ugly, you could see them eyes'a his. And they was diff'rent.

Dan, that's my stepdad, has all these boys come over to our house. He calls 'em business friends, or somethin'. They got these nice clothes and smell like perfume like 'em Mexicans workin' down by the dock. But, the Junk Man, to me he was always cleaner, like those crystal glasses been in the family since before anyone can recall. Ours was in the attic with all the other old stuff. Ma was always tellin' us to watch out for 'em when we was up there. You know, they're all dirty and dusty, but underneath they look so nice if you clean 'em. I did once, when Gran'ma came over for Christmas. Only a few, 'cause Ma said there's no point in doin' 'em all. But when you wash 'em, they look like diamonds, and you can thump 'em and it's like a bell. Well, that's what I thought 'bout the Junk Man, sometimes. He was like a crystal glass, just dirty and all.

I was just lookin' at him huntin' through the garbage. It must've been ten minutes, and I didn't move or say nothin'. But he turned 'round and looked at me and smiled, like he'd knowed I was there the whole time!

"Hey, boy. You called Josh, right?" Was what he said.

Well, 'ats sorta what he said. I s'ppose you're gonna have to pretend a bit and b'lieve me when I talk for him. Not that I'm makin' it up and tellin' you a lie, 'cause it's all true, I swear. But the Junk Man had such a funny way of sayin' things, like no man ever did. You should'a heard it and then you'd know and see why I can't really tell you right. All his words don't come out much like he said 'em. But I gotta try as best I can to tell you.

So, like I was sayin', he said, "Hey, boy. You called Josh, right?"

Well, him knowin' my name was too much, and I was gonna run off, but his eyes they kept me lookin', somehow. He weren't comin' over or nothin', but you can't be hangin' near too many types, you know, and he was for dang sure a type. But like I said, it was those eyes of his that made me feel OK, like nothin' bad was gonna happen. You ain't seen those eyes, and there ain't no use in tryin' to tell you 'cause you'd think I was crazy or somethin'. But they was some eyes, all peaceful like. I ain't knowed nobody with peaceful eyes. You might, I s'ppose.

Well, so I said, "How come you know my name?" He smiled, and I saw that he was missin' a bunch of teeth.

He said, "I live here, boy, and I see all you come and go." Then, he went back to pickin' through the trash. He had a big bag on the ground full of stuff, and he kept droppin' things from the trash piles into it. I asked him what he was doin', but he wouldn't answer, and just looked over his shoulder and made a sound at me and closed up his bag all secret-like and walked off.

Well, I almost lost him, then. There was a hundred reasons just to leave and go home and forget I ever did see him, but you know that's not what happened, or else I wouldn't be here tellin' you this story. I got up my courage and ran after him. The Trash Yard is like a house-a-mirrors and ev'rythin' looks the same no matter where you go. Well, 'less you look real hard.

So, I mightta never found him, but I did, and I came out to some open place that didn't look like ev'rythin' else. You should'a seen it, seen it before they bulldozed it, 'cause it would'a made your eyes pop out 'cause it ain't like nothin' in no junk yard or anywhere else, I bet. A real diff'rent place and all because of the Junk Man, 'cause he was the one, you know, that took all the trash and laid it out and planted the garden and made that museum, 'cause he saw it diff'rent, saw it all like it was new.

So, if you hadda seen it, seen the walkway he made out of old broke things, seen all 'em plants - flowers and tomaters and such - seen how it was all laid out just right, and 'specially if you seen the museum, well, then you'd know what I was talkin' 'bout and you'd b'lieve me more'an I bet you do now. 'Cause I ain't makin' it up, that I swear. And when I came out on it, runnin' after him, well, I knowed somethin' was up, and that it was like I came to a side path on the road goin' someplace new, someplace special, like from a book 'bout some other faraway place.

But I couldn't see all that I told you right at first when I came out to that small clearin' where the piles stopped and I saw that ol' rusty house he was livin' in.

I saw some of it, like when you're drivin' past somethin' on the highway, and it was all such a sight I stopped runnin' and just stared. Too long, I reckon, 'cause before I knowed it, he seen me and it was too late to hide or nothin'. Well, he laughed and tossed that sack on the ground and waved me on over.

Well, I came this far, so I figured I might as well see it out. I went on up to him, I reckon a bit scared like 'cause he said, "Don't be scared. I ain't gonna hurt you." I looked at him and then down to see what I could see in that bag.

"Now, what you reckon I got in this bag?"

Well, I didn't know, like I told you, so I said, "I reckon you got a lot'a junk." Boy, that sure set him off, and one'a his eyebrows jumped near off his forehead. He didn't have no other eyebrow on the other side, just kinda a long trench in the skin where it oughtta be.

"*Junk*? No, boy! Ain't no junk in here."

So, he opened up the bag and poured out all that was in it. And it was full of junk. I ain't lyin'. There was all sorts of trinkets and old clothes and worst of all, old food and stuff that just stunk. So, I told him what I thought, that it was just a bunch of smelly old junk.

"Boy, it ain't junk 'less you throws it out. It might be junk to somebody, but look! I ain't throwin' it out, no Sir. I'm takin' it in! See? Do you *see*, boy?" and he gave me this real hard look like I'd better see 'cause it was real impor'ant and the whole world was gonna end if I didn't see it like he did. Well, I could see he was takin' it in, but I saw that he was takin' in junk. So, I told him.

"You go to school?" I said yes. "Well, they sho' don't teach you much there. If you take it in, how's it still gonna be junk? Like when you took in that stray dog. Yes Sir, I seen you. You gotta be careful with 'em strays. But you picked him right. He's a good dog. This bag full is like a part of you, right by yo' heart." He reached up and was tappin' his chest. "Don't fo'get that. It ain't no junk. *Never.*"

I still didn't understand what he was meanin', and then's where I figured he must be part crazy. Maybe his brain was gettin' full'a holes like his face, or maybe he was like that man in the movie 'bout a bird's nest who got his brain cut up so that he can't talk or nothin.' Well, I ain't sayin' the Junk Man had his brain cut up or couldn't talk, 'cause he could, oftentimes too much really for my own likin', but he might one day, 'cause he might be crazy like that man, so that some folk would'a wanted to cut on him to shut him up.

I thought that lots'a times, and even argued with myself whether he was or not. Crazy, I mean. I never did figure it out. Now I figure, since I liked him so much, that if he was crazy then I must be too, least partly. If I'm crazy, well then I want to be crazy like the Junk Man, 'cause his way is a good way to be. He weren't crazy like 'em homeless in the park. Most of 'em got a look in their eye like somethin's been cut up in their head. The Junk Man was diff'rent, and his eyes, like I told you before, was all diff'rent. And 'sides, you ain't never heard'a no homeless man who made a house, or a museum, right?

Well, that just goes to show you - the Junk Man weren't sick like 'em other homeless, and he weren't sick like ev'rybody else who's a-goin' through life pretendin' to be happy but hatin' ev'rything.

Anyways, I think he saw that he weren't makin' no sense to me, so he shook his head. "You ain't b'lievin' me, boy. Well, come on and see fo' yo'self."

He started dividin' up all that junk first - all the old rotten food in one pile with all those flies, trinkets in another, bottles, rocks in another, and a few special things in a small pile on the side. Then, he went inside his house and came out with a big bowl, two buckets, and some round-end sticks. Well, he went to work on the rotten food first. It was an awful big pile, and he took some and put it into the bowls and mashed it up with the sticks.

Over and over he did, and it weren't easy, I reckon, 'cause he was workin' hard and sweat was drippin' down his face, poolin' in all 'em leper creases and holes. After he mashed up a bowlful, he'd dump it to the side and dig out some dirt and mix it up with the old food. He kept doin' this 'til all the old food was mashed up and mixed up with dirt, 'til it looked like some awful green puddin' or somethin'. Then, he put it into the two buckets.

"Come, boy," he said and walked to that garden he had. I swear, we walked by a hundred diff'rent kinda plants, and half of 'em I didn't even know even though I growed up on Pa's farm. He took those buckets to a clear patch next to some watermellons, where a lot of the dirt was dug up, likely with a shovel he had on the ground close by.

"Befo' I plant a new patch," he told me, "I always soup up the ground, give it some flavor so the seeds'll take to it," and he smiled at me and laughed. Then, he poured the green puddin' into all 'em little trenches he made, and stirred up the whole ground real good, and I mean it looked like some work! Afterwards, he looked a bit tired, and rested up on the handle of the shovel.

"We gotta wait'a while. Then, the ground'll be ready."

And he wiped off his hands on his torn jeans and walked back to the front of the garden where he left the other piles. He filled the buckets with bits of bottles and stones and broke concrete and carried 'em off to the walkway that ran up to his house. Near the end of the walkway, where it stopped, he poured out the junk. I asked him what he was doin'.

"I gonna run it all the way 'round. So it'll go up and 'round the house. Take me a good year, I figure, but it'll look real nice at the end."

"You gonna use that junk?"

"What you reckon I been doin', boy?"

Then, I finally looked close at the walkway, and sure 'nuff, I could see how it had all kinda diff'rent stones and bits of glass in it, all flattened and polished flat as good as concrete, or nearly. And I wondered how he'd done that, made it so nice, like he was somebody or somethin' and not just some ugly leper livin' in the Trash Yard. But he went back to the piles again, and I had to run to keep up.

"What are you gonna do with 'em clothes?"

"Some might fit me, and those that don't, I'm usin' the cloth to make mo' clothes or mend what I got."

"So, what's 'at pile there, 'at little one," I asked him. I s'ppose I was gettin' real int'rested in all that stuff.

"That's the most special of all, boy. Look at it now, close!"

So, I did. But I didn't see much. Well, there was a shiny gold button and some old pit'cher in a frame and some tore-up book. But it didn't seem all that special to me, and I told him that.

"Then, you ain't lookin' hard 'nuff. All this goes to the museum, boy, *all* this." Then, he was real quiet, lookin' down at the junk almost sad like, not sayin' nothin' for a while, so I asked him 'bout the museum.

"One you ain't gonna see. Not yet, no how. You ain't ready. Now, go home and leave me be," and he took 'em clothes and that pile and went up his walkway and closed the door to his shack.

Well, that was it. That's how I met the Junk Man. I went home then, 'cause it was late and Ma would likely as not light into me for draggin' myself in like a tomcat. That's what she says when I come home late. But that's what started it, me and the Junk Man, I mean. All the rest I think growed up from that day, like a seed he planted in his garden. Well, 'til all those sons of bitches rode over it.

Sorry for cussin'. My Pa cussed up a storm and Ma always lit into him for it, and said God didn't have no place in heaven for a man talkin' such filth. So, I s'ppose I ought'a stop cussin', but it always sets me off to think on it, even though Mr. Robertson said it was for the best, for me and the Junk Man. But I don't b'lieve in that for a minute, and all 'em lousy men who don't know nothin' 'bout it can go to hell 'less God forgive 'em, like Ma says. God'll forgive 'em, but I don't see how.

3

So, after that me and the Junk Man came to be real good friends. I went to see him near ev'ry other day, and soon he was lettin' me help him with the gatherin' and some with the fixin' up a things 'round his place. He didn't pay me nothin', and I doubt he ever hadda dime, 'cept maybe when he was a kid like me and his Ma gave him somethin'.

But I helped him 'cause it was like helpin' a friend, or maybe like helpin' someone who you knowed was your good friend, even though the Junk Man ain't really done nothin' for me. But I always felt like he did, or was 'bout to, and I always felt kinda grateful for somethin' that I never got, or thought I got. Well, don't ask me to explain it - maybe it was just I saw a nice adventure to have for a while. It was sure better than home or school, that I can tell you. And listenin' to his stories weren't too bad, neither.

But I had to be careful. I had to make sure that there weren't nobody wise to what I was doin'. So, I couldn't go ev'ry day, even if I wanted to. Somedays, I was just with my friends and doin' stuff with 'em. And that's what I told my Ma ev'ryday 'bout what I was up to. "Playin' with Toby, Ma. OK, Ma, I'll be back before dark." You know, like that and all, even if I weren't goin' to play with Toby or some friends or anyone else. And it was hard not comin' home lookin' or smellin' like I been in the Trash Yard. I reckon it's good that boys are always comin' home full with filth, like my Ma says, 'cause it sure helped keepin' the Trash Yard a secret. And I never took no one with me to see the Junk Man. Not one time, even if Toby saw him once by accident.

I s'ppose my fav'rit part, that thing that was always pullin' me back, mor'an his garden or museum even, was buildin' that walkway. Right early on the Junk Man let me help with that, and it was great seein' it get bigger and all ev'ry week. The done parts I walked over ev'ry day, knowin' that I'd put it all there myself, with my own hands.

The best part was puttin' in the stones and polished glass. First, we'd collect all the stuff the Junk Man took back from the Trash Yard, and like I told you, split it up into diff'rent piles. Well, one pile was only for the walkway, and it was broke glass and rocks and marble and such. Well, part of my job was polishin' it all up so that it was nice for the walkway. The Junk Man showed me how. Then, when they was ready, the Junk Man would come by with the mixture. I never did get to find out what that was, but it looked like wet concrete, but it set diff'rent and took longer to get hard, and it didn't have all 'em little holes you see in most concrete. And the best of all, it sparkled, like the Junk Man throwed in a million tiny pieces'a glass like stars.

Well, like stars in the country, not the city. City lights just wash all the stars outta the sky at night. Well, he'd pour it out, 'tween the wood he set to hold it in the right shape when it was still wet and soft, and then he'd flatten it out with some old tools he made from the junk, or some folk tossed out that he'd fix up. Then, I'd go through and add all the polished stuff, and he'd smooth it out so that in the end it was flat but with the polished glass and stones and all sparklin'. Like a king's walkway more'an the Junk Man's. Like that for a king from a story.

One day he came by when I was polishin' stuff and said, "Hey, boy! Look here ev'ryone, Josh himself's a-sittin' here, and what might you be doin', boy?"

I said I was polishin' old broke glass and dirty stones, which I didn't need to be sayin', 'cause it was clear to any ol' fool what I was doin'. Seein' as there weren't no one there but me and him, it weren't makin' no sense for him to be askin' like there was. And since I came here 'bout ev'ry day, there weren't no sense for the Junk Man to be askin' me. But him bein' crazy, there weren't always a reason for what he was sayin'.

"No Sir, you're makin' diamonds! Don't you know? Sparklin' diamonds like stars fallin' out the sky," and he laughed and walked off someplace else.

Well, I ain't never thought of it that way. But real diamonds, well, I read one time in a book at school that they come from rocks in mountains, all trapped inside the rocks. And men had to cut 'em out just right or they'd be ruined, and then they had to cut 'em pretty wearin' special glasses and all to see real good.

So, I s'ppose the Junk Man was right in a way. I was takin' stuff buried in the trash and bringin' out all I could to make it pretty, even if there weren't no need of special glasses and such. The Junk Man showed me how and gave me all the tools, and it was nice, you know, to take some old, dirty broke up trash and make it into a sparklin' thing, and then set it out in the walkway, so that on sunny days you could look at it, like a river goin' 'round his shack, and the thing sparkled up like a real river when the sun is shinin' down on the water.

That's one thing I miss maybe the most of all 'bout leavin' the mountains for the city. Them small streams runnin' clean, not all green and awful smellin' like the rivers here, with clear water you can drink and the sound of the water runnin' over the rocks. I could lis'en to it, like the wind hittin' up against the trees, almost all day I think.

Don't get me wrong, I ain't sayin' it was always easy up there. I weren't likin' the winter so much on account of me and Tom hadda sleep up in the attic. That old attic was full a stuff like I told ya, dusty and such, and you ain't got no room to move or do nothin' up there. But that weren't the worst of it. It'd get hot oftentimes in the summer, but not like down here in the city. Up in the mountains, 'em summers weren't so bad.

But 'em winters 'bout killed you sometimes, 'specially as that old house ain't got no heatin' 'cept for the fireplace downstairs. Here, they got pipes and stuff bringin' heat all over. But me and my brother had to sleep up in that attic. I can't tell you how cold that was. I'd stay down as long as I could near that fire 'til Pa made us go up. Then, I'd wrap as many clothes 'round me as I could. The inside of my nose would freeze up there, and if I had a glass of water, it was ice by mornin'.

But it was awful nice in the summer, sittin' there by 'em little rivers and the sun lightin' up on the water and the water talkin' on the rocks. But that's all gone now and there ain't nothin' here but concrete and metal and water that's like what you flush down the toilet when you done your business. Metal and rust. And trash. Lots'a that. Not much like the forest and streams. So, I miss 'at. That's maybe another reason why I liked the walkway so much. 'Cause sometimes it looked like a real live river.

I miss havin' a dog too. Ma says where we was livin' in the city they don't take to people havin' no pets. Even dogs. I tried to take in a dog one time I found with no collar one day. But we had to get ridda it. At the old house we had a bunch'a dogs. Some was smarter'an all hell. Some was good huntin' dogs. My fav'rit was this big ol' German shepherd we called

Wolf 'cause he was lookin' like a big ol' wild wolf. He was 'bout smart like a person, I swear.

One time when Tom and me was both'rin' this wild pig, and it started in to chasin' us all over, which was scary like you wouldn't know 'less you had one of 'em things gruntin' and snortin' behind you with 'em sharp tusks and all. Well, old Wolf heard all that commotion and came runnin' over and made that pig chase him around so we'd get safe. Then, he ran inside the big barn and came runnin' out soon afterwards, and I'll be if he didn't close that barn door, trappin' that pig inside!

I swear that's what happened, and you can go believin' me or not, whichever you like. But that's the truth. We ran and told Pa, and he came out with his gun and blasted that ol' pig right in the head. We cooked him up and ate him for 'bout three days, I reckon. After he shot the thing he said to Wolf, "Good dawg," which was what he was.

But Bingo, well, he was mostly dumb. Dumb name too, after that song. You know which one I mean. That's on account of my brother, that name. I used to think it was that name as made that dog so dumb, but I don't think that no more. Some things are just dumb, and there ain't no reason. Like some folk just born mean.

Bingo was a little black scotlan' terror. He was always pickin' fights with bigger dogs and such. I recall one time when this collie was puttin' her paw on his head, keepin' him down, and he was just barkin' like crazy and tryin' to go fight her. But she just kept that paw on his head, holdin' him down 'til he got too tired.

Well, he was gettin' in so much trouble with 'em neighbors dogs that Pa kept him on a leash on our porch. Well, when Pa did that I reckon he weren't figurin' on how dumb that dog was, or maybe he'd a found a safer way. That dog hated bein' tied up and was always runnin' from one side to the other, 'specially when he was hearin' other dogs barkin'.

Well, that's how he did it. One time he must'a gone right off 'at porch, which was a bit high to the ground, and with that leash just hung hisself. I found him comin' home from school, just a-hangin' there, his tongue rolled out and his mouth all open with his eyes bugged out. But I weren't too sad. Well, I guess a little. But, like I said, he was a right dumb dog.

But I'd be lyin' if I told you 'em streams or dogs or anythin' else was what I most liked 'bout the country. It weren't my Pa neither, even if'n I do miss him, but I ain't missin' so much gettin' hit all the time 'cross the head. And I really ain't missin' that leather belt of his, which you can imagine hurt like the devil.

I miss playin' with my brother Tom out in 'em woods, I s'ppose. I reckon I do miss that lots. But only in the daytime. When I lived out there, I was littler, and I was pretty scared of the dark. So was Tom. So we didn't play none at night, even if my Ma would'a let us. I mean, I didn't even like to feed that old dumb pony, Trigger. He was dumb, even if he did unlock the gate and 'scape sometimes. I mean, I was ridin' him in the woods one time and does he stop and go around 'em low branches? No Sir, he just went right on through. Well, it weren't both'rin' him none, I s'ppose, even if they was hittin' me in the head and knockin' me right off to the ground.

Dumb old pony. So, I didn't care to try hard to make sure his bucket didn't spill over or nothin' when I was feedin' him. When it came dark, I'd fill the bucket with feed and tear on out the door fast as I could to the fence. I swear I could feel 'em monsters growin' behind me like ghosts, like cold air blowin' on my back, gettin' closer. So, when I'd get to that fence, I'd just throw that bucket right over, hardly lookin' where it landed. Then, since I knowed there weren't much time left, as I'd been out there so long givin' 'em monsters lots of time to get close and catch up to me, I'd run back even faster to the house so when I got there my heart was 'bout to explode in me and I couldn't hardly breathe.

Yeah, I had a right bad fear'a monsters. I knowed even then it was mostly all growin' outta my mind, but bein' scared's stronger'an thinkin' straight, I reckon. Like you might know. I think the worst was after I saw that mud monster on TV. Maybe you seen that. He came outta the swamp and was all made of mud and killed people. They burned him with salt at the end of it, 'cept for his hand, which even if it didn't have no body no more was still crawlin' by itself.

Well, that made it so I was lyin' 'wake at nights after that in my bed seein' that hand comin' in the door or outside the winda over my head. That was bad, havin' a winda over your head where 'em monsters could'a come in so easy at night when Ma and Pa was sleepin' and get you before you could even yell out or nothin'. Yeah, I hated that winda, and the closet right next to it, 'cause you know, there ain't no tellin' what kinda things was waitin' in there, neither.

Well, so it ain't no wonder really I loved Ria, even if there was lots of other reasons to love her. Like for one, she was 'bout the nicest person in the whole world, and would sing songs 'bout lemon trees and such on her guitar. Yeah, I s'ppose maybe more'an all 'em other things I miss maybe Ria the most, her nice smile and nice way with me and Tom. She was my cousin, but to be truthful I don't recall exactly how. But that don't matter. One thing I recall most was how she was always tryin' to help me when she came over not be so scared at nights. Singin' songs and sittin' by my bed. She was a lot bigger'n us then, I think a teenager when I was just ten or somethin'.

Anyways, the best story was the one 'bout all'em good monsters. The way she told it was like you had a bunch of good monsters who would all be friends and who liked little kids like us. And they was always holdin' hands and dancin' and singin' outside at night protectin' us from 'em bad ones. She said 'cause of 'em, we ain't never gotta be a-feared of 'em bad ones. And you know, what when she was there, sittin' by the bed and tellin' us such stories, I weren't scared no more, and oftentimes even went to sleep not worryin' 'bout any'a those things I always did.

Well, she was somethin' special, but she's still out in the country, and I don't know what she's doin' now. So, it's good I ain't so scared of monsters no more, 'cause there ain't Ria 'round to sit by my bed and tell me stories and make all'em bad things go away.

Well, anyway, that's where we was before. Now, I'm in the city, and lots of times with the Junk Man, helpin' out like I told you. But I weren't only helpin'. We used to talk lots, 'bout all kinda things, and he was always real sure of hisself, and told me how things were s'pposed to be and how I was s'pposed to act, like he was my Ma or some preacher.

Now, I ain't holden no grudge 'gainst him for that, and anyways, lotta what he said was good sense, seein' where it was comin' from. A man livin' in the Trash Yard, I mean. I shouldn't say I didn't lis'en to what he said, 'cause I did. Even if he was oftentimes just plain a fool 'bout things. He just didn't understand the world real good, all hid away from it, and he thought we all should act nicer to ev'rybody, which I think so too, but ain't no one gonna do it, so you might as well know it and keep your distance and your fists ready. "Can't trust nothin' but the bullet from yer own gun – an' 'at's only when yer holdin' it," Pa used to say, and he was right. So, even if the Junk Man said all kinda nice things, since I knowed better, I just lis'ened but knowed what was right and what was bull.

It weren't so bad bein' 'round him, and I was startin' to wait for times I could go to see him, like I used to wait for school to be out or a ball game. Since I was helpin' with the plants and the collectin' and the walkway, buildin' that with my own hands, well, since I did all that I felt like a part of it, like I kinda belonged there, if you follow me. I wouldn't say that to nobody, 'cause they wouldn't understand. Likely you don't, neither, but that was what it was.

Yeah, the Junk Man was someone you could get to like real good, or least I could. He ain't never done nothin' to make fun a me or steal or lie or nothin' like that. Ain't like no one else. Even my friends. It's like ev'ryone's gotta keep ev'ryone else on a leash like a dog, so even your friends gotta pull out a knife and cut you, even when you ain't done nothin' wrong. The way I figure, that's meanin' none of us, we ain't really got no friends. Whatever they say or you wantin' to b'lieve. 'Cause what friend's it that cuts you just for bein'? 'Less you want to say that's all the friends. Which is what I'm saying, I reckon.

I mean, I ain't sayin' we was always agreein' and happy together. No Sir, sometimes we'd see things for diff'rent, and he was always preachin' like I said. But most people preach 'cause they gotta have you see ev'rythin' like they do, like it scares 'em if someone, even some dumb kid like me who can't even read so good, well, it scares 'em if you got diff'rent ideas 'bout what's good and bad. Naw, the Junk Man weren't like that. Scared, I mean. He was just so goddamn sure he knowed what was and what weren't, and he told you so for your own good. You could argue with him for a while, but then he'd say somethin' like, "Well, you do what you gotta do, boy. The Good Lord knows what's best."

Now, I knowed all kinda people, like that Mr. Robertson, who told me what's best and seem all worried 'bout me. But I'll bet you, it ain't like they was really worried 'bout me, you know, what's really me. They got all kinda int'rest in some thing in their heads they callin' me. Heck, half the time they tellin' me this or that they ain't even lookin' at me!

He weren't like that, the Junk Man. He was always lookin' in my eyes, even if it was kinda funny, or even kinda scary sometimes. I just felt like he was seein' me for what I was. Which is scary, but good, really, as there ain't no more fence between you and no pretendin'.

4

Well, finally I s'ppose I passed some test'a his and he figured I was ready to see the museum he'd been tellin' me 'bout for so long but never let me get nowheres near. Like I said, it wasn't much to look at on the outside, just a tent made from some old sheets and plastic to keep the water out when it rained, but once you got inside and he told you what each thing was about, well, it was really somethin' special. It was like goin' to a new place that no one ain't ever been to.

I mean, I've seen 'em statues in the city museums and all 'em pit'chers. Heck, I even saw some'a that modern art, which 'tween you and me looks like it was drawn by a bunch of drunk chickens with their feet dipped in paint. I don't know what fool paid his money for that, but I weren't tricked one dang bit, let me tell you. But somebody's got a good thing goin'there.

Some'a the other stuff was pretty and all, and I wondered how a person could'a learned himself to cut up hard rock like it was wood and bring out some pretty girl with nice boobs and all. But after all it never left me with nothin' to take back. I mean, it was like candy, if you know what I mean - you ain't gonna be full, 'less you eat so much that you get sick, and that ain't no good kinda full, as you know. So, I weren't much for 'em art museums.

But the Junk Man, well, he had somethin' else. There weren't nothin' so pretty in it like a marble statue or some angels painted up nice, but you hadda see his art and know the story, then it all made sense in a way nothin' else in those other museums ever did. I mean, look, you might'a even thought it was some modern art stuff, all that junk set up and put out like he wanted, but it weren't that, no Sir. The Junk Man always told you the story.

There was so much there that a person could see, and I wish now I'd a told some others 'bout it so they could see it, too. I mean, it was somethin' special, and now that it's all plowed under the ground no one's ever gonna see it again, which is a crime, really. So, I s'ppose that's one reason I'm here tellin' you this, 'cause it's still in my mind, and the Junk Man's, wherever he is. So, maybe I can tell the story to you before it's all gone forever. The problem's that my mem'ry ain't the best, and I forget stuff less that hits me hardest, if you know what I'm sayin'. And while ev'rythin' in that museum was worth a thousand times that city stuff, some was more special than the others. So, I won't lie to you - I'm only gonna be able to tell you a part of all he had, even if that's a shame. Somethin' makes me feel like it's mostly what I didn't see, or can't recall no more, that was most'a what was impor'ant. But I'm just some kid, so the Good Lord will forgive me forgettin'.

So, anyway, one day while we was plantin' some flowers 'round the shack, I asked again 'bout the museum, like I did at least ev'ry other day I was there, if you want to know the truth. Well, he 'bout makes me drop the plants I was holdin' and said, "You been real patient, boy. Why don't we have a look inside after we finish this."

Sure 'nuff, when we'd done finished he took me through his house, and out the back door where it opened to the museum. First time I saw it, it looked like some funny flea market with little tables and stools set all 'round. But on ev'ry piece of furn'ture was some ol' junk he found in the Trash Yard and cleaned up and put up like it was art for all to see. He took me through it all and told me 'bout each one, and they all had a sad story. I don't know why he was collectin' junk from sad stories, and to be honest, I don't know how he thought he knowed 'em stories 'bout all that stuff. So, I asked him.

"Like I told you befo', boy, it's all in the lookin'. You ain't seein' nothin' 'cause you ain't lookin', not really lookin', anyways. It's right there in front like the sun."

Well, I looked but I still couldn't see no stories. But, like I said, I half b'lieved he was crazy anyway, so I didn't let that bother me. So, I asked him to tell me the stories. And you know, I ain't ever gonna know if'n any of 'em was true, but I don't care, 'cause they just as well could'a been, and I liked to hear it all.

So, we went on back inside the museum. And under that tent he made it was dark like it gets when a heavy rain blocks out most'a the sun. But the Junk Man, he tore open parts, fine like with a knife, so light'd come in on the things inside. Sometimes, he'd open one up and cover it with some ol' shirt or somethin', so it hadda light half way 'tween the dark and the bright light. Things like that. I reckon all that was for his art, you know, 'cause 'em artists are always foolin' with the light and gettin' it just right and such. And that's what the Junk Man did.

So, anyways, your eyes had to get used to it, but then you'd see it all. And it was like a magic act, 'cause I swear there was more room inside than there could'a ever been from the size of that little tent outside. It was like the things he found and made into his art just went on forever back through under that tent so that it was like some giant ol' barn. I mean, I saw lots of things in that museum, but I didn't see all of it, and I swear it looked like I could'a walked a whole hour to the end of it. I don't know how he managed that. Like he'd been collectin' this stuff a hundred years or somethin'. Maybe a thing with 'em lights and all, so then you'd see under it all the things he made, one after the other, stretchin' back 'til you was dizzy. I reckon it was right then that I knowed this was for real a magic place, that'd it stay with me 'til I was dead. Maybe even after, when I got to be an angel, if you believin' what the preacher man says. Maybe if'n 'em angels are rememb'rin' what they was before.

Not sure I'm b'lievin' all that to tell the truth, even if it'd be nice to be an angel with wings and go to heaven. But I ain't never seen no angels, and it's hard b'lievin' all that the preacher's sayin', even if he's got the Good Book and all. They was right good stories, don't get me wrong, but there ain't no way some man gonna fit all 'em animals on one boat or one fish gonna feed all 'em people and such. So, that got me to askin' where the Good Book came from, and the preacher said from God. And I asked how'd he know? And he said I had to b'lieve. So, I asked why I hadda b'lieve what he was tellin' me? And he said 'cause he told the Truth that was the Word of God. And I asked how I'd know he was for real knowin' the Word of God, and he said 'cause it was from the Good Book. Well, that stopped me, as I couldn't find no way to argue 'gainst that, even if it was seemin' like I couldn't find no way to hold onto them answers.

Anyway, that first day the Junk Man took me through and showed me all 'em things, one after th'other, tellin' me their stories and all so that it was dark when I got home and Ma let me have it. And I forgot half'a what he said, to tell you the truth. But there was some that kinda stayed with me, so that I'd keep thinkin' on 'em even when I weren't there with him, and those was the ones I was always goin' back to look at, and the ones I recalls good enough to tell you.

First, there was his Two Trees. That's how he called it. I always called it The Crutches. There was two young trees, growed up hardly seven or eight feet, planted right close together. And they was hooked up to a set of strange crutches, for some cripple, made all outta metal with two circles at the top where your arms could go through when they was used. That way they wouldn't go under your arms, I s'ppose, like normal crutches. The two trees was a-growin' up through 'em circles, and the metal legs'a the crutches was stuck in the ground close to the roots. The tree must'a been tied up on the crutches like a cripple, I reckon, so as when they was weak and young they could grow up straight and tall.

"They was belongin' to a soldier," said the Junk Man. "He lost his legs fightin' in a war."

"He lost both his legs?"

"Not all of 'em, mostly under the knee. Blowed off by a lan' mine."

"Damn," was what I said.

"He woke up one mornin' in the hospital bed with some pretty young thing changin' his bloody bandages where there was stumps like sawed off branches, and a doctor tellin' him he weren't never gonna be walkin' no mo'. No Sir, weren't gonna walk again on 'em legs, well, 'cept on these here crutches." And he pointed over to 'em holdin' the trees.

"He came home a cripple, with folk he didn't know yellin' at him at the airport, and his own folk not even wantin' to talk to him. They 'specially didn't like lookin' at him. Metal from that mine tore open his face, you see. They never got it back together right." The Junk Man was shakin' his head.

"He came home after givin' his legs and found they didn't want the resta him no mo'. Not at the fact'ry, so he was a cripple with no job. Found his woman didn't see him so beaut'ful no mo', so he lost her, too. Po' boy didn't keep much. Well, he tried fo' a few years. Tried hard, livin' off folk, the gov'ment. But his heart got tired, and he didn't have nothin' mo' to give. So, he left 'em crutches, left 'em in some broke-down shelter, crawled himself out down to the dock. He lis'ened to 'em bells ringin' on the boats for a good half'a day. Then, he pushed on off to the water, where not havin' no legs made sure he weren't comin' back up. The folks runnin' the shelters, well, they ain't got no use fo' no crutches, so they just throwed 'em out the next mornin'. Gotta send 'em on over to the Junk Man."

Well, as you can rightly guess, that was 'bout the saddest story I ever heard, even if it was just all made up in that crazy head of the Junk Man. And I looked at 'em crutches again and saw how the trees at the top crossed over each other and then growed up straight again, and close to where they was gonna push up against the tent, the Junk Man cut two holes, one for each'a the trees, so they could keep on growin', and get sun, I s'ppose. And the sun bein' high then in the sky outside made light come down straight like white columns on 'em trees and crutches, and the dust was swirlin' in the light like 'em glass snowballs old women are always collectin' in their livin' rooms.

"See, boy, they be growin' strong, straight an' tall," he said, meanin' 'em trees he planted. "Yes Sir, soon they be too thick for 'em crutches, and gonna bust open 'em metal rings. After, they gonna grow themselves, and 'em crutches gonna fall over to the side. They won't be needin' 'em no mo'."

I looked and saw that he was likely right. Them trunks was gettin' thick. I bet soon they weren't gonna need 'em crutches, just like he said. But the Junk Man was already movin' over to another thing in the museum.

Over on one side was a shape like a man, all dressed up and leanin' over a book. It was only some old mannequin somebody threw out, dressed up in old funny clothes. The book was big, and on the side I could read Hamlet in fancy gold letterin'. The mannequin had his hand up, like he was makin' a speech, and his foot with some funny pointy shoe was on top'a some ol' broke wine bottle, like it was smashin' it in front'a your eyes. The Junk Man cut a bunch'a holes in the tarp, big ones with cardboard like little tunnels in the holes. That made it so the light didn't spread out so much and it looked like spot lights like they use for 'em school plays.

The Junk Man said all that stuff was some ol' man's who died a drunk in a hospital with a tube stuck down his throat not able to tell his family how he was sorry for makin' their life a hell. He told me lots 'bout how drinkin' can ruin a man, but I didn't lis'en so close 'cause I knowed all 'bout that 'cause our neighbor, Mr. Patterson, well, he's drunk all the time. That family ain't got nothin' on account'a him. Ma says he drinks up all their money. I always see the kids beggin' him to go and take 'em to school in the mornin's. Their Ma works a lot, I s'ppose 'cause he don't, and he's s'ppose to do things like take 'em to school and whatnot. But he don't seem even to do that s'good. Ma says they was once rich folks who lost ev'rythin' 'cause'a that no good drunk. So, now they was poor like us. But I reckon it's harder to be poor after you been rich. When you're poor like me, you ain't never had no mansion or big car or swimmin' pool, so when your Pa drunk it all away and lost his job and ev'rythin' there really ain't so much to miss after it's gone, if you see what I'm sayin'.

Anyway, the Junk Man said that man was an actor. Said he loved gettin' in front of all kind'a people and actin', and that he loved to sing too and such all things I never was so good at or liked doin'. Said he started a playhouse for kids in the city, and that hospitals for war heroes and all asked him to come sing for 'em.

"But that bottle tore it all down, boy," he said. "He tried runnin' with the high crowd after he made it big. But the po' man ain't knowed he had the weakness. Maybe didn't wanna know. Not 'til it was too late and he was a drunk and tore himself and his family down to nothin'. An' 'em high flyin' friends left like ghosts. He ain't never see'd 'em no mo' after his money run out."

"He lived a drunk fo' thirty years, 'til he died. His chil'ren hated him, and so did his woman, even if she stayed with him 'til her heart gave out fo' carryin' the family and mo'. She'd beat him some nights when he was drunk, so much hate inside her fo' what he'd done to 'em, and how he kept on a-doin' it. One night she took him back from that club, where he did lotsa his drinkin', and when he got out the car he fell down and out like a light. So, she rolled him down the hill to the porch and left him there that night. Rolled him over the concrete and grass and dirt and just left him outside. Like a dog."

"In the end he got mo' and mo' sick, his feet swellin' up like balloons so as his toenails was comin' off. The doctor said he hadda stop drinkin', lose weight and all, or he'd lose 'em feet. They'd have to cut 'em right off. But he told the doc to go to the devil. Well, he went on, even after his wife died and his daughter was takin' care a man she hated and wished she mighta loved. But his body was fallin' to pieces, and soon he was lyin' in that hospital bed, breathin' only 'cause some machine made him breathe, lookin' outta some plastic tent with yella eyes oozin'. There was his daughter and her sons, his own gran'chil'ren, lookin' at him like he was some kinda monster. They felt sorry fo' him 'cause he was dyin', but they didn't want to be gettin' too close."

The Junk Man pointed at the broken glass. "An' that bottle, well, it was gone, now. No mo' to take the pain away. Yes Sir, the end was the hardest, 'cause he woke up to a life that was a bad dream he made, woke up after thirty years a-sleepin' in the bottle, woke up strapped to a machine and dyin' and feelin' like some hated creature."

Then, the Junk Man looked over at me and I saw he had tears runnin' down his cheeks. But his voice was the same. "Ain't no way to live, and it ain't no way to die. An' there was nothin' but pain fo' alla 'em at the end. Them kids never got free of that life, that whole thing."

Then, he walked up to the mannequin, which he told me was wearin' old costumes from his playhouse days, and told me he put him up like that 'cause the only time this man ever did somethin' good for others was when he was actin', and he put his foot over the broke bottle as a kinda hope for winnin' over such things as bein' a drunk.

But I was thinkin', and I'm still thinkin' that now, that the Junk Man was too much for dreamin'. I mean, it's nice and all to hope for winnin' out over 'em things, but you know what, I ain't never seen no one do it. All I ever seen is folk messin' stuff up and breakin' it and throwin' it out so that nothin' ever got fixed right. And in my own thinkin', it weren't no man ever over a broke bottle like he made it look. I'd bet it'd be more real if'n he stacked up lots'a bottles over broke men, or mannequins, or whatever.

But, well, that's the Junk Man for you. We're all breakin' and throwin' out, and he's always takin' it in and tryin' to fix it. I reckon that's why he's livin' in his trash world and we're all out in the city where it seems there ain't no use in dreamin' like that.

The next one we saw was maybe the most curious of 'em all. Well, for me anyways, and not 'cause there was curious things in it or nothin', but mainly 'cause it was all nice things you wouldn't think of seein' in a place like this, the Junk Man's museum. And when it all went with the story, well, it was like a dream where everthin' is real and fits together but don't make the least bitta sense.

What I mean is, when you was there lookin' and hearin' the story, maybe it made some sense. But after you left and went home, then it weren't so clear no more. Like a dream. You know, when you're havin' it, or maybe right after wakin' up, all that craziness don't bother you none. But after you get up and pee or walk around or eat somethin', and you think back on that dream, you wonder how anybody'd ever think it weren't nothin' but crazy.

So, there was a nice Dumbo carpet with a Winnie-the-pooh lamp, and light from a hole in the tarp shinin' like the lamp was on, down on the middle of it. And all around in a circle, almost holdin' hands like, you might've counted up fifty stuffed animals. You know, like little kids are always sleepin' with or cartin' around and suckin' their thumbs. Or even their fingers – like my brother, he never sucked his thumb, only his finger. Really. We got a pit'cher I can show you if you don't b'lieve me. He had this big ol' callus on it from rubbin' it on his teeth. He was always wantin' you to hold his foot when he was tired too, another funny thing. Never could sleep without Ma holdin' his foot. Now, you explain that to me.

Anyway, a bunch'a stuffed animals. There was one el'phant, red with a big letter A on his side for 'Bama, and a monkey missin' a hand, a dog, like a puppy golden retriever, all scruffed up with no eyes and a neck 'bout ready to tear so that the head would come right off. A big ball, too. Big, stuffed ball bigger 'an any stuffed animal, with diff'rent colored patches all over. I wonder what kinda kid slept with a ball. I ain't never seen that. I can't rightly recall all of 'em. It was like a bunch of kids came in with their animals and set 'em all up and just left. Scary, really, 'specially with that light shinin' down on 'em in that dark tent and all. So, 'course I asked him what all that was for.

"They was throwed out by a man who lost his little girl."

"She died?"

"Well, no. Not really, but there's ways to lose someone that's just like to dyin'. Sometimes worse, 'cause you knowin' they ain't really gone, it's just you can't get to 'em. Hurts like to dyin'. See 'em animals? They was her fav'rits. Fo' a long time she had 'em, 'cause she was slow, what some callin' retarded. Well, maybe she weren't so wise in the world as most, but, boy, she hadda good heart. A pretty smile too, and she was nicer'an any you might ever meet. Just ask her cousins. When she was a young woman, they was small kids, maybe six or seven, and she'd care for 'em sometimes. Well, mostly just play with 'em. She liked playin' with 'em, and they loved her. They'd tell you now, even if they be growed and married off. They recall her happy face, how nice she was. How she loved 'em. An' they won't tell you things like that 'bout too many people they knowed, no Sir."

"So, how come her Pa throwed 'em animals out? They too old?"

"No, he was heart broke, po' man. Didn't wanna have 'em 'round the house no mo'. Too many mem'ries. His girl was gone, you see. She was always fallin' into trouble, played 'round by some mo' clever'an her. One bad man after the other, and there was nothin' her daddy could do. An' then, the last man came. He took her 'way fo' good. She was puttin' out a house fulla chil'ren, but her daddy never saw one gran'chile. That man of hers wouldn't have nothin' to do with him, and kept her locked up, sad, makin' babies. So, he throwed all 'em toys out one day, lasta all her fav'rits, which I got right here," he said, wavin' his hand around the circle, shakin' his head like he was sad, too.

"What happened in the end?" I asked him.

"End? There ain't no end to things like that, even if many wishin' for an end that don't come."

Then he stopped, and turned 'round and got right up near my face, starin' with his eyes real big at me. "See, boy, they's waitin' fo' her, them animals. Waitin' fo' her to come on back home. An' they ain't never gonna lose hope." Then, he smiled with that bumpy ol' puffed-up face, like he was all a'sudden happy. *Crazy*, like I said.

Well, we saw a bunch more that day and other days, but I forgot lots of 'em. Sorry 'bout that, if you was int'rested, which I bet you ain't so much. I bet if I was sittin' with you and some poor kid like me was tellin' this story, it wouldn't come over so int'restin'. But that ain't no fault of the Junk Man or the museum. I bet if you'd seen the real thing, and heard it from the Junk Man, it'd seem more int'restin'. Yeah, I'd bet a lot of money on that.

But I ain't the Junk Man, so I ought to get to those things that go with the story, and since I started it all by tellin' you 'bout how I ruined ev'rythin' by talkin' 'bout that Alter Rose, maybe you'd be int'rested in that.

Well, in the middle was the main part, on some ol' table, a glass bowl fulla dirt with a small rose bush that always kept one rose, all by itself, in the same place, no matter when I came, like it was some magic bush or somethin'. I don't know if it ever died, or if he just kept puttin' new ones in. But it seemed like the same bush, maybe 'cause I only saw it a few times. I don't know, but he might've been prunin' it, so a new one was always growin' there.

Anyway, like I said, in this bowl was the rose, and kinda threaded like one 'em wicker baskets through the stem, right 'neath the petals, was a gold ring like a spider web. Filigree he called it, hangin' there without fallin'. And it was somethin' special to see too, let me tell you, 'cause he had it just right so that the sun comin' through 'em holes in the tarp was always catchin' it, and it was tossin' back the sunbeams to whoever was lookin', sparklin' up like stars. He must'a spent I don't know how long gettin' that just right.

That ring was somethin' magic. The Junk Man said, "I found it lyin' in a corner, 'bout drowned in some ol' rotten egg that stunk like you never knowed," and he laughed somethin' awful. "But it was there, half stickin' outta that egg, so that the sun catched the gold, and that's what turned my eye."

The filigree was right pretty, like I said, maybe like curtains at gran'ma's, but with gold lace. Like you'd taken some string and laced it all up pretty, and turned it to gold. It sure was a site and I only saw one other thing like it in my whole life.

He said, "A young boy, not much older'an you, gave it to his sweetheart," and he winked at me, laughin' real hard with that wheeze a'his. He was always laughin' hard. "Funny boy, he was. First *true* love, like they's a-sayin' in the movies. Too bad fo' him it was true, and befo' he knowed much 'bout that pretty girl, he was givin' over his heart and soul and body and ev'rythin' else to her. Never got 'em back, neither," he said, just shakin' his head. "She throwed that ring away one day."

"Why'd she do that?" I asked him.

"She figured she didn't love him no mo'."

Well, if I ain't knowed 'bout my Ma and Pa, that'd be hard to b'lieve. I mean, I got lotsa friends, but none of 'em ever gave me no nice ring like that. If they did, I promise you I'd be their best friend, forever. Well, I s'ppose it'd seem like that in the beginnin'. 'Cause after Ma and Pa splittin' up, I s'ppose I know better that there ain't nothin' gonna last forever. But I was still wonderin'.

"Naw," I said, "She must'a lost it."

"No, she throwed it out, I'm tellin' you. I'm seein' her face right now when she done it. Somethin' set hard, a kinda question runnin' 'cross it like a wind. Sometimes blowin', most the time, just quiet."

That's *crazy*, right? That don't make not one bit a sense. Well, I knowed it *weren't* crazy, 'cause I knowed a story like it, but I didn't say nothin' then. I'd bring it to him later. But I did want to know 'bout that girl. After that girl and me was doin' it in the Trash Yard, after I came to be a man and all, well, I thought after her sometimes. And other girls, wonderin' what it might be like to do that and other things with 'em, only then they wouldn't go away and not come back, and we might be friends and go around and see things together. Stuff like that.

'Sides, I have this dream. Ever since I was little, really. In the dream I'm always walkin' 'round lookin' for this girl. She's pretty and all, but that ain't why I'm lookin' for her. To tell you, I never know why I'm lookin' for her. But I know I need her, need to find her, like everythin' else 'round me don't matter, and it ain't real and only she is. But ev'rywhere I go there are all these signs sayin' "she's here" and such, but she's never there. I always wake up with this pit'cher of her face in my head. Ain't never found her in 'em dreams.

So, I asked him, "What she look like?"

The Junk Man smiled. "She was a beauty, boy. Had a face like a scup'ture made'a china, with blue eyes like the clear sky. Yes Sir, and she had hair that was brown and gold all mixed up, with a circle, like a crown, hair 'round her face lit yella like gold. Face like an angel," he said, starin' off not lookin' at nothin'. "That boy never understood what happened. Now, he's lost. Too much'a his life, lost, like a great part'a him stayed with her. And he's always lookin', seein' her face in crowds, in dreams, never findin' her. Never fillin' up what was taken out," he said.

"How you know all this, you knowed her?"

He laughed real hard at what I said. "No, boy. I see it in my mind's eyes. Like I see all 'em that lives in the junk."

Crazy ol' leper was what he was, but he sure told a great story. Anyways, those two together, that rose and that ring, like gold cobwebs restin' on red carpet, was mighty pretty. But the most curious part, the part that seemed to tie it all together, was that hair. Real hair from some other young girl, he told me.

"She was suff'rin' from the cancer," he said one day when he led me through. "It was in her blood, growin' in her lungs, like some evil creature." He shook his head like he was sad again and could see her right in front of him. "She was a fine dancer, pretty girl, and clever. Fancy ballets and floatin' on the air like a swan. But that cancer stole her breath, and she couldn't dance no mo'. An' the doctors, well, they put on airs like the prophets, but they ain't had nothin' to give her but poison."

He bent over all secret like, starin' down on me.

"See, boy, you gotta take that poison in a little at a time, and make so' you stay 'live a little longer than that cancer. 'Bout kills most folk, and it took her hair. That poison sank deep, right to the roots and they shriveled up, and died. An' boy, let me tell you, it was a loss. She had right pretty hair, long like a river to her waist, soft and fine like silk. An' it just fell right out to the floor. Her mamma cleaned it up and throwed it out with the rest of the trash."

He was quiet for a minute. Lost faraway off thinkin' 'bout this pretty young dancin' girl. Then he said, "An' it come to me. All 'em things find me one way or the other, 'less they was born outta somethin' dark and mean."

I don't know what he did with that hair, how he made it into what it was, like some rich lady's scarf or blanket for diamonds or somethin', but it was all wrapped 'round the Alter Rose, from the table up all 'round the bowl and stem to the very top, and the rose seemed like it was lyin' at the top on that silk hair like it was restin' on a bed and the ring lit up right pretty with all her lost hair behind it and the light comin' in just right, like I said before.

It was like nothin' you ever saw, or like nothin' I ever saw before or after, anyways. I don't s'ppose I seen too much, but I'd bet you all I got that there ain't nothin' in no museum anywhere or even in that French museum that'll beat that Alter Rose for somethin' pretty. If there is, well, I want to see it too, someday.

5

So, you see, I finally did get to see that museum. That's how lucky I was. Likely as not you ain't thinkin' so, but for myself I think I'm 'bout the luckiest person ever lived to get to see it. It was like bein' in a movie. Well, kinda. I mean in a movie things ain't like real life. Things are all put there just right, and so much is happ'nin' and nothin' 'tween it all borin' and such like ev'ryday for real. Movies always got 'em excitin' things one after the other, with music and such makin' it all feel good. I mean, don't get me wrong, I'd pay for a movie any ol' day over a real day life. That's why we're all runnin' to see 'em movies, right?

Oftentimes real life's got excitin' stuff, but even then since you're in it, it still ain't like no movie. I mean, you can get all scared in a movie, but that ain't nothin' like really bein' scared. That's how it feels to me, anyways. And I've knowed a lot of that excitement.

I s'ppose nothin' beat leavin' Pa for bein' like a movie for my own life. We tried two times before we made it. First time, Ma was dumb and called him from the house when he was at work tellin' him we was leavin'. That was after he throwed her head against the bedpost one night. She was gettin' scared of him more and more after each beatin'. Can't blame her for that. I figured Pa could'a killed us if we did somethin' too bad that he weren't likin'. One time he got mad at me and throwed a shovel 'cross the air like a boomerang. 'Bout took my head off. He was like that oftentimes when he was real mad. I was right scared'a him, anyway.

So, after she called him, we finished packin' up and got in the car and drove off. But after Ma called, Pa got in his truck and tore on over, so before we even got off the dirt road to the big road, he got there. He turned his truck 'round sideways and blocked the whole road, so Ma had nowhere to go. So, there we was sittin' stuck on that road with all 'em suitcases and Ma up front and me and Tom in the back not knowin' what was gonna happen. But Pa weren't into beatin' on us out in public, and he talked all quiet like to Ma and in the end we turned 'round and went home and unpacked all 'em suitcases. And I don't think Pa hit her afterwards again for a good while.

But 'course the next time it was just worse, like always. That was the first time I saw my Ma with a busted nose and a ugly old black eye, and we didn't go nowhere for a whole week, not even to school. And we had to make up all these lies to ev'ryone 'bout why we was at home so long. Well, it weren't long after that time that Ma and us left for good. I think mainly on account of my gran'ma.

I think Ma was too scared to leave just herself, but gran'ma kinda pushed her into it 'cause she's 'bout as scary as Pa. But Ma did it right this time, hi'rin' two men to come on out and protect us if Pa catched wind of the whole thing, even though he didn't since Ma was smarter and didn't call him this time. They was these two big ol' men, who said they could wait in the bushes for Pa to come home and break his legs if Ma wanted 'em to. I think they was hopin' Ma'd say yes, but she didn't, lookin' all sad. Which I was happy 'bout, 'cause even if Pa was beatin' on us and Ma so much, I didn't much want 'em two big men breakin' his legs.

Our Aunt Betty came out to help us. She had this ol' ugly orange car that Ma buyed off her later on. We loaded up the cars and drove on out, and Pa never knowed 'bout it 'til he came home, I s'ppose.

But that weren't the end of it. It gets more in'trestin' 'cause Pa found out where we was stayin' in the new town, comes drivin' up and goes yellin' at Ma at her new job. Well, first he went over to gran'mas to find out where Ma went and got all bellig'rent with her when she wouldn't tell him. But gran'ma, well she's the toughest of the whole fam'ly, and she pulled out a shotgun and told him she was gonna fill him up with it 'less'n he cleared off, which he did. But he found Ma, anyhow. She ran outta her new job and to her car and was gonna drive off, but Pa jumps on the hood and's a-hangin' on through all the traffic. Well, that's what my Ma said, anyways. I weren't there. Like in the movies, she said. You know, or that TV show stuff. At the end, police pull 'em over and 'cuff Pa and haul him off to jail. That were fine'ly the end with it, and Pa never bothered us no more. Truth is, I ain't never seen him after that.

So, you might say we had our bit with the excitement. But I s'ppose so do most fam'lies if'n they'd fess up. Maybe not. Maybe s'just my folks so messed up. Well, not I s'ppose if half what the Junk Man's sayin's true. I don't s'ppose you ever had 'em kinda troubles.

Oftentimes, I'd think it just weren't right for God to give us all 'em troubles. But I don't s'ppose I deserve much better, anyhow. God likely got mad at me lots of times. Like when Tom and I was messin' with 'em cats. I don't know why we did that, and I'd never do it now, but then we weren't carin'. Don't know why. Don't know why I changed so that it seems so bad a thing to do now. I s'ppose kids are kinda dumb 'bout some things, and have to grow up to get smarter, even if you see some big folks that still doin' mean things like pickin' on animals.

But we was hard on 'em cats. Sometimes, we'd put 'em in the brick Bar-B-Q and close 'em in with the old rusty iron gratin'. They'd be all meowin' and scared. Others, we'd take 'em out and sling 'em around by their paws and then let 'em go flyin' through the air. Then, we'd hunt 'em down again and drop 'em in a big pile'a leaves we'd raked up, so they sinked to the pile bottom and hadda dig their way up. We'd watch 'em do that. It weren't like we was glad they'd be hurtin' or scared or nothin'. It was more like it was funny or somethin'. Like they was toys. I s'ppose we weren't thinkin' 'bout how it might be feelin' if'n we was those cats and some kids was slingin' us 'round and dumpin' us and such. I s'ppose it was mean, really. I'd never do somethin' like that now, but I did once. So, I know God's got it in for me on account of that and other things.

That's maybe why I liked the Junk Man, 'cause he stopped me thinkin' so down on ev'rythin' that'd happen to me or someone else. I mean, look at what he was doin' with all that throwed out broke and dirty old junk. I told him that one time.

"You sure got a way of turnin' broke junk into somethin' fine," I said. But he looked at me in a funny way.

"Ain't easy, boy, not one bit's easy, and some's worse'an others," he said lookin' far off, like he was thinkin' 'bout somethin' that's hard to see.

"Like what?" I asked.

"Like what?" He said, turnin' to give me a hard look. "You seen bad, boy, but there's worse that even the Junk Man don't know how he's ever gonna fix. You ain't seen what's happened to some chil'ren, bein' killed, or worse, or dyin' fo' no food. You ain't seen folk tied to a machine to have life drained out to make gold for a few. You ain't seen far'way lands, where the Devil opened his Pit, and evil spirits took holda men and they ran 'cross the lands like monsters, doin' evil so dark it ain't fit for speakin'. No, boy, you ain't seen even worse. Some folk livin' but walkin' like dead, and wantin' to be dead, so they won't know no mo' the world and what it's done to 'em. But it ain't fo' you to know, and nothin' you might do with it, nohow. Yes Sir, the Lord A'mighty's savin' it all fo' the Junk Man." And he looked up to the blue sky like he was talkin' with God himself.

"That why you ain't got nothin' like that here, in the museum?"

"Had befo'. At another place. Ain't come 'cross no real hard case here yet, but I ain't really been here that long, you see."

But I was too s'prised to ask more 'bout 'em hard cases. "You been somewhere else doin' all this?"

He gave me one of those looks again, like he was tellin' a secret I knowed but pretended I didn't. "Well, don't you know it, I been all over, 'cross the whole world. Ain't nothin' nowhere gonna hold the Junk Man. But they always tryin'. Yes, Sir! Soon as the root's taken, well, they hunt me down, and dig it up. Ain't you never heard this story 'bout me?" he said lookin' a bit upset.

I didn't want to say I hadn't, and that I bet no one else had, neither. There weren't really no point in arguin' with him when he got like this, crazy, like I said, like he was famous and ev'rybody knowed 'bout him and his big ideas 'bout him and the world and talkin' to God and all that. So, I just looked away, tryin' to think how this old bent leper, without a dime really and no job or nothin', would ever think he was livin' all over the world and such. I ain't sayin' he was lyin', just sometimes crazy, so that he couldn't help talkin' like that.

And I s'ppose I didn't want to think too much on it, when you came down to it. 'Cause I was worryin' 'bout myself, to tell you the truth. Maybe crazy thinkin' is like that lep'rosy that you can catch if it's 'round too much, gettin' inside your head. You see, I was startin' to have right curious ideas after spendin' so much time with him. Maybe when folk are close, like best friends, not to be sayin' he was my best friend, even if'n I was with him now more'an other friends. I reckon after spendin' so much time with the Junk Man, you might say he was close to bein' like a best friend, if that could be, 'cause it's hard to figure, really, when you think 'bout what he was. I s'ppose it's too bad he looked and talked like he did, 'cause if he'd looked diff'rent, and maybe talked more like that Mr. Robertson, well, maybe they'd a left him alone. But maybe I ain't thinkin' right, 'cause, well, then he wouldn't be the Junk Man no more, I reckon.

Anyway, like I said, it was these curious ideas I was gettin' that had me worried 'bout goin' crazy like him. Half-crazy ideas, like daydreams, where he was the one who was good and right and the whole world, leastways 'em like Mr. Robertson and the police and all 'em that went after him, they was what was wrong, even though if you didn't know nothin' it might look diff'rent. In my dream he was all over, goin' here and there, fixin' things, and they was tryin' to snuff him out like a fire, or some weed you tear out but more's always growin' back.

But that ain't right either, really, 'cause it makes him sound wrong. Maybe like he was a light, like a spot light or a bright summer day sun, and they hated havin' him around, so they put on sunglasses and made dark houses and with no windas and tried all kinda things to keep it out. And in the end they didn't see no sun at all, but all the time it really was still high in the sky, shinin' like always. Well, at least for those things that had a use for it.

Sorry - it don't make no sense what I'm sayin'. I ain't one for explainin' somethin' so hard. It don't make no sense to me, neither.

But I liked to lis'en to the Junk Man. He made things quiet-like inside me. Like that pink house in the country I walked by ev'ry day, where that girl was always playin' the piano. She never knowed but I'd go sneakin' up to her winda and lis'en somedays, 'cause that music made me feel all quiet and peaceful inside. And that's a right nice thing.

6

I reckon I ought to get 'round now to tellin' you 'bout how it all ended up 'tween me and the Junk Man. Well, I s'ppose really just how it all ended up for the Junk Man, 'cause, as you can see yourself, I'm still here, and there ain't much that's changed in my life. Well, not much changed so that any old person could see it, anyways. 'Cause I reckon I'm diff'rent. I don't s'ppose nobody'd go through all I did - you know, workin' with the Junk man, bein', I reckon, his friend, seein' that museum, and then all that they did to it - well, that's all bound to change somethin', even if I ain't so clear on what it might be, 'sides feelin' diff'rent and maybe seein' things sometimes diff'rent. But no matter what, they ended it just dead, startin' with that Mr. Robertson.

After I let it all slip out and was so plum stupid to talk 'bout him, they didn't leave me be 'bout it all. I s'ppose they didn't leave him be, neither. That Mr.

Robertson, he kept me in that couns'lin' room 'bout the whole day it seemed, and called Ma at the end and was talkin' all quiet like to others in the Main Office. Well, they didn't even let me go home by myself that day, and my Ma came drivin' up, lookin' all worried and lost, and her and Mr. Robertson started talkin'.

And then he started tellin' Ma how I was with this homeless man ev'ryday, and nobody knowed who he was and where he came from, and what kinda man he was. It weren't just what he said, but how he said it. I learned then that you can say somethin' two ways and have it sound like you said two diff'rent things, even if the words don't change. Yeah, he was sayin' things in a way that made it sound real bad. And it weren't no use for me to say nothin'. Nobody lis'ens to no kid, anyway. Then, Mr. Robertson and Ma went off and talked together where I couldn't hear.

It weren't 'til we was on the way home that my Ma even said somethin' 'bout it all to me. And you might guess that by then I was 'bout scared outta my shorts. But she didn't yell at me or nothin', not at the first, but she was talkin' all quiet like, like maybe she was scared or somethin', which, you know, just made the whole thing even scarier.

"Mr. Robertson tol' me somethin' 'bout where ya been goin' these days after school and the weekends," she said. I didn't say nothin', but just stared out the winda watchin' stuff go by.

"Well, Josh, 'at all true, what he was sayin'?"

" 'Bout what?" I said, knowin' all the time what she was meanin'.

" 'Bout ya goin' off t'at landfill and stayin' w'at crazy, homeless leper!"

"He ain't crazy, Ma!" I said, even if, like I told you myself, I was thinkin' he was kinda crazy. But Ma was startin' to get worked up.

"Hush up, young man! Yer in a heap'a trouble. What was ya thinkin'? Ain't ya got nothin' in 'at head a yers? Ain't Ah learned ya nothin'? My own boy with filthy trash - 'bout makes me sick!"

"Ma, he ain't like that."

"Like 'at? Ya gonna tell me 'bout those homeless? 'Bout some leper sick with it and spreadin' it 'round? Ya don't know nothin'! Ah don't care what 'ese city folk are sayin', 'ere ain't no good in those homeless. And God didn't strike him down so'as we'd be minglin' with 'at sin! Josh, ya know better'n'at!"

"He ain't like that," I said again, not really knowin' what else to say, as I couldn't think so well with Ma yellin' at me. That's what always happens when she starts into yellin' at me, there ain't no use thinkin' 'cause I get all twisted up like, and my stomach gets sick. Makes me feel like a baby, but it's like she got some power over me and there ain't nothin' I could do. But all this was 'bout killin' me to hear all 'em things said 'bout the Junk Man and I was just tryin' not to bust out cryin' over it all like a baby.

"Ma, he ain't like that. We're friends."

"No, y'ain't! Not no more! Don't ya never say nothin' so hurtful to yer Ma 'gain. My son ain't no friend with no filthy leper, ya hear? An' ya never gonna be!"

"But I am, Ma!"

"Don't ya talk back to me, young man!"

"But Ma," I said, cryin' alright like a damn baby. "You don't know him. He takes the trash and cleans it up, makes it all pretty and grows nice things from it all."

"Shut yer mouth this instant!"

And I did, 'cause she was gettin' like she was when you better not be sayin' another word, 'cause, well, if I wanted to stand up for myself and the Junk Man, I'd have to break through somethin' awful. I don't know, but I think if'n I ever did that I'd break somethin' 'tween my Ma and me. So, I shut up, and tried to clean up my face. And we was quiet for a long time.

Then she started again, but in that quiet voice I was hatin'. "Mr. Robertson was sayin' ya been up in his house. 'At true, Josh?"

"Yes, Ma'am," was what I said.

"Whutcha do there?"

Well, I didn't feel like tellin' her 'bout the museum and all, 'specially as she weren't never gonna understand none'a it. Nothin' t'all. So, I just said, "Nothin' much," which weren't the right thing to say, as I found out quick.

"Whutcha mean, nothin' much? Whutcha tellin' me, 'atchu been up t'at place near ev'ry day, ev'ry day when Ah thought ya was playin' out with yer friends like ya said ya was, an' ya weren't doin' nothin'? Ya think yer ma's stupid? Ya hidin' somethin', boy? Tell me that! Whutcha hidin', Josh?"

And she was all mad and crazy like, and I was right scared, 'cause I didn't know it was comin' on so fast, and since I was hidin' everythin' 'bout the museum, I feared she done caught me, that Mr. Robertson must'a told her 'bout all that back at the school. So, I figured I hadda fess up.

"It weren't nothin' much, Ma. We was only goin' through his museum and stuff." But it was like she weren't hearin' nothin' I said.

"Have ya been sinnin', a-doin' things ya shouldn't, things the Devil would take ya straightta hell fer? Tell me that!"

"Ma…" I said not knowin' what she was gettin' on about. But she just kept on yellin'.

"He touch ya? Don't ya tell me no lie – 'at whutcha was doin' in'at house? With 'at leper like an abom'nation to God?!"

"Whutcha mean, Ma?" I said, not knowin' then what she meant 'cause I didn't know so much 'bout all 'em fags and stuff 'til Toby told me 'bout it.

"Jist wait 'til we git home, and we'll see what Dan says 'bout this!"

So, we didn't say nothin' more 'til we got home, and then Ma told Dan ev'rythin', least 'bout some idea she had 'bout what happened. But Dan weren't none too happy to be hearin' it, and my guess is that he'd'a rather been some place else not hearin' nothin' 'bout it than sittin' where he was, with Ma walkin' and yellin' all around the house, and him sittin' there tryin' to look like he was my Pa or somethin'.

Dan ain't got no real kids, not his own, just me and Tom from Ma, and he ain't got no sense in bein' like Pa. Now Pa, likely as not he would'a knocked me 'cross the head with his hand or somethin', more'an likely pulled off his belt and whipped me good, and that would'a been the end of it. With Pa, there weren't much need for words. But Dan, well, he just looked real sick and didn't say much, which course just upset Ma more, so that when she was done yellin' she had lost most'a her voice.

It weren't long, I s'ppose, 'til the whole world knowed 'bout me and the Junk Man, and half of 'em thought we was fags, I reckon or somthin'. We had that Mr. Robertson even comin' over to our house, if you could b'lieve that, and more, doctors and teachers with him. They asked me the same questions, lookin' at me like they knowed somethin' 'bout what I was sayin' that I didn't. Well, they didn't know nothin', far as I'm concerned, and never once lis'ened to what I was tellin' 'em. So, I don't know what they was good for, 'less it was tryin' to make the whole thing they was buildin' up look big and impor'ant. And they was sure good at that.

Mostly, I was tryin' to stay out of it all, hangin' around downstairs and playin' with our cats. I s'ppose I didn't tell you 'bout them. Well, like I said, we weren't s'pposed to have no pets, but one night this cat comes to our door and lies down and won't leave.

She's bigger 'an heck and Ma says she's pregnant. We took her in and that night she squirts out five kittens.

That was pretty crazy thing to see, to tell you the truth. They come out in these sacks and the mom cat tears 'em off and eats 'em! Then, she licks the cats and they drink milk from her. Well, except for one that she didn't tear that sack off, so my Ma did, and instead of havin' a gray or white cat like the others, there was a black cat, smaller'n all the rest. Well, even after we took off that sack she wouldn't feed it, and Ma fed it with a straw she blocked up at one end with her finger. It was always the smallest and last to do things like climb up the stairs and stuff. Funny things, those cats. They used to sleep on my Ma's head at night, on top of her rollers and all that she uses to make her hair curly.

Anyway, I was playin' with 'em cats a lot, 'cause that was before Ma gave'm all away to some farm. I heard they all died of some cat disease later on. But we still had'em then, when the whole big problem with the Junk Man came about, before they died and Ma went down to the basement and all them fleas that been starvin' weeks covered her legs 'til they was black and she screamed like someone was killin' her down there.

But cats or not, there weren't no hidin'. That's another thing I learned after all this. When I was a kid, I always b'lieved you could hide from monsters and such. Maybe they'd find you in the end, maybe not, but there was always the idea of it, like a hope. But that's a kid's way of thinkin' 'bout the world, and it ain't real. I reckon you know that, but I just learned it. I s'ppose what's real are other kinda bad things like monsters but not lookin' like monsters, maybe even lookin' like people, even like right good proper people, and there ain't no hidin' from 'em.

So, soon after there came the day that ended it all, really. I s'ppose I should'a seen it comin' with all 'em questions and how it was clear as day - they had it in for the Junk Man. And that makes me sad, 'cause maybe if I'd seen it comin', I could'a said somethin' to him to tell him they was a-comin' after him, so he'd hide or run off someplace new. He might just'a stayed there waitin' for 'em in the end, no matter what I said. That'd be like him. He might'a got some fool idea in his head 'bout the whole thing. Anyway, it would'a made me feel a whole lot better if I did at least say somethin'. But I was just all a-shook up by ev'rythin', how they was all actin', I mean.

When you get down to it, I s'ppose I was just thinkin' 'bout myself and weren't really carin' so much 'bout the ol' Junk Man. Reckon that's all for bein' so scared and all. I'm startin' to think that bein' scared's the worst thing a person can do. Wors'en hurtin' cats or lyin' or drinkin' or other bad things. 'Cause bein' scared turns you into somethin' you ain't most'a the time, and takes all your good things away, and any chance to think right 'bout things.

Yeah, being scared's I think's maybe part of all those and other bad things. I b'lieve that maybe 'cause'a what it did to me. Bein' scared made me forget ev'rythin' good and what I owed the Junk Man.

That's what makes me the most sad, I s'ppose, that after all we done I just run off and forgot about him in the end. That ain't like no real friend, and I reckon I just weren't one.

7

So, there came the day and I knowed somethin' was up just 'cause how it was the first day nobody said nothin' 'bout it all. It was like it never happened. But I heard Ma on the phone, whisperrin' and changin' her talk if I ever got close enough to hear. And somethin' just weren't sittin' right in my insides, to tell you the truth. So, I worked up my courage and asked her what was happ'nin' and why no one wanted to talk no more 'bout the Junk Man, 'cause I knowed somehow he was why no one was talkin'.

Well, she weren't gonna say nothin', but that I wasn't to talk no more 'bout him, and that they was fixin' to take care of that problem. That problem bein' the Junk Man, I reckoned. You can guess what she meant, and so did I somehow, and I figured then and there that I finally had to go say somethin' to him, even if they had to kill me for goin' there again.

So, after supper I sneaked out, and I ran fast to the Trash Yard, and even before I got there I saw 'em flashin' lights from the police cars, all bright blue and red in the night, lightin' up off the scrap metal. There was police and other cars, even dogs, and I saw Mr. Robertson and our principal, Mr. Jones talkin' to some police, and that old man Morris standin' there lookin' half asleep and lost. It weren't so hard to understand what was happ'nin'. They was comin' for the Junk Man, and more'an likely I was too late to help him.

My heart was kickin' in my chest, and I wanted to scream out, but I knowed that wouldn't do no good, so I ran over to the side fence, where the hole was I told you 'bout before, and crawled in. Then, I ran to the shack. But I was right. I was too late. There was police all over - outside, inside the shack and the museum, and they made a mess out of all the plants and things around the door. But the Junk Man weren't there.

It was like a bad dream, you know, when you can't never get where you need and fix what went wrong or save somebody, and I was 'bout choked up now, scared and sad and I don't know what else, knowin' all the time that they must'a just took him. I stood there half a minute, hidin' behind some junk, not knowin' what to do. Then, I figured they might have him up by the front'a the Trash Yard, so I ran back there, not hidin' no more and just hopin' I might find him before he was gone forever, 'cause I ain't even said goodbye.

Well, that was how they catched me, them police, just when I was gettin' there. A big man took hold'a me by my shirt and asked who I was and what I was doin' there. Then, Mr. Robertson saw me too, and looked all s'prised and worried, and started walkin' over real fast and yellin' stuff 'bout how he knowed me to the policeman.

And then, I saw him. Two police had him all handcuffed, like he was a crim'nal or was gonna hurt someone, and they was takin' him to a police truck. Well, I s'ppose I just couldn't stand it no more, and since that policeman who was holdin' my shirt was lookin' at Mr. Robertson comin' over, it weren't hard for me to break free, which is what I did. I ran to the Junk Man, callin' him and yellin' that I was sorry and cryin' and I don't even know what else, and I didn't even make it over, 'cause more police ran up and grabbed me, even though I was kickin' and screamin' somethin' awful.

"Get that monster outta here!" one said, pointin' over at the Junk Man.

And then I heard the Junk Man, and I looked over and he was starin' right at me, all calm like, and he said, "Don't be scared, Josh. They taken me befo'. But I always come back, don't you worry none. They ain't never kept me mo'an a few days. I always come back to the trash, boy, yes Sir, don't you be doubtin' the Junk Man!"

He said all that while they was yellin' at him to shut up, and pushin' him hard so that he was 'bout fallin' down, even though he was old, like I said, and had 'em missin' toes from being a leper and all. But they didn't care 'bout that. Like it didn't matter if'n he was old or they hurt him. Those police and alla 'em didn't even care.

But he weren't done talkin', and he broke free and held up his ol' gnarly hands, even all cuffed up. I don't know how he did that. And I couldn't b'lieve it, but they stopped. Ev'rythin' stopped. And he looked at 'em all, with this hard look like he was seein' right through 'em. And he talked at the last, like it was to ev'rybody, not just me no more, and it was like the whole world stopped and lis'ened.

"Just what ya'll reckon yo' *doin'*? I'm the *Junk Man*. Don't you know who I am? It's *yo'* trash I'm takin' somewheres else, feedin' my garden. It's all *ya'll* broke makin' my art."

Then, he shook his head at 'em, like they was school kids and he was some teacher.

"But I'm seein' the same as ever in yo' eyes. They's empty, not seein' nothin'! So, ya'll still ain't gonna learn, is you? No matter what the Junk Man say. That's a shame, but I know you can't help it. Ain't nobody can see the trash like the Junk Man. No Sirs, the Junk Man's gotta see it *fo'* you. Whutcha gonna do when I'm gone? Who's gonna look fo' you? Who you gonna find to fix all that you broke?"

I felt like I couldn't breathe, like I wasn't even there no more. Like I was floatin' over it all and watchin' all of it from some other place.

"Ain't no one, I'm tellin' you. It all gonna just lie there broke up on the ground, waitin' 'til another day.

'Til that day the Junk Man gonna come back. Come back again, and fix it."

And he was standin' so tall then when he said all that, not bent like normal, with all 'em red and blue lights spinnin' around makin' me dizzy, and he said that so loud and strong. Well, for a few seconds, ev'ryone, even those police pushin' him around, they was just stopped and lookin' at him, not sayin' nothin'. Like they was froze and all the world was lis'enin' to the Junk Man talk.

But it was just a second only, and some wind picked up, and blowed 'round all the Trash Yard dirt. Then, they all pushed him inside that truck and drived off. And that's the last time I ever seen him.

8

I got to ride back home after all that in a police car, but it weren't so much fun as I always thought it'd be. And like I told you it would happen, I was just 'bout killed for goin' there. But I didn't care. The next few days I didn't care much 'bout nothin', and didn't talk to nobody. I reckon I was too sad, really. It was a kinda sad I ain't never knowed before. Kind like bein' dead weren't gonna be no worse.

I think my Ma felt kinda bad 'bout how I was feelin', 'cause she stopped bein' so mad and started tryin' hard to make me happy, bein' extra nice and cookin' me all kinda things I like. But I didn't want none of it, and I didn't get more happy. I was just empty like a poured out bucket.

Maybe, it was like havin' a kinda fever. That's somethin' I was always havin' trouble with, 'em fevers. My Ma said that when I was a kid, I was always runnin' hot when I got sick. Once, they thought I was 'bout dead when I was a baby since I got so hot and weren't eatin' or cryin' or nothin'. Pa shook me 'round like a dead possum's what they told me, but I didn't do nothin'. Too sick with the fever.

We didn't have any thermometers lyin' 'round where we used to live. So, we didn't know nothin' 'bout how hot we was gettin'. But one time after we moved, I got a fever again, and Ma had one of 'em thermometers from the store, and she said I was 106, which was real bad, I s'ppose. She checked me with it because I was so hot and was talkin' 'bout kids playin' football in the room with me when there weren't none. And 'cause I said my brother Tom painted all our furn'ture green. She said when you get a bad fever you turn crazy and see stuff ain't there and such. I remember some'a them old women near the Trail sayin' how that's when devils and angels are a-fighin' for your soul. So, she throwed me in a tub'a cold water to cool me down like a boiled egg. I recall bein' in there, havin' the shakes like you can't imagine. But I don't recall those boys playin' football or that green furn'ture.

Anyway, I reckon the first thing that got me more to bein' my old self was gettin' mad. First, I was nothin' but sad, and not sad really, 'cause there weren't much cryin' and the like. But, like I said, feelin' nothin' really, all empty like I was missin' somethin' and just walkin' around like sleepin' or lyin' down like

I had a fever. But then I started to wake up, and I was madder'an all hell. But there ain't nothin' a kid can do when he's mad at grownups, so I'd just walk 'round mad and hatin' ev'rything.

Pretty soon I was findin' my way back to the Trash Yard. It weren't like I was gonna get in trouble, 'cause they'd never catch me, and 'sides, after they took him away, nobody cared no more what I did or where I went. Just like before. Before I opened my dumb ol' mouth and ruined it all.

You know, I had to go back, really. Maybe you can understand. But I might'a been better off if'n I just stayed away and never went back to that ol' Trash Yard, 'cause when I got back to his place, they'd knocked it all down. Tore up all his plants, or bulldozed 'em under, and they'd knocked down his shack and the museum. They didn't leave nothin', not even that pretty walkway I helped make. Like they wanted to make it like it never was, like there never was somethin' pretty made from all 'at garbage, like all 'em broke things never got made nice. I have a mind they were wantin' it so as there never was no Junk Man at all. So, they made sure and left nothin'.

Nothin' at all. I looked hard for things, for that Alter Rose, or those crutches, for anythin'. 'Specially the heart necklace. I s'ppose I still ain't told you 'bout that. Well, there's so much to tell, I reckon I forgot. The heart necklace, that's what I gave to the Junk Man, for the museum. It was my Ma's one time, before she throwed it out. He'd just 'bout finished puttin' it up, in its own place like it was special like the other stuff, but they took him and knocked it all down and buried that heart necklace in the dirt so that I'll never find it now. I looked a bunch of days, but it weren't no use. If you ain't never seen what a good bulldozer can do to a place, it's hard to understand. It'll change all the land, so it looks like some diff'rent place, even if you know it ain't.

When we lived out with Pa, I saw a whole acre bulldozed. That was on account of the big fire Pa let loose and nearly burned down all the land and the neighbors' houses and our house, too. He was clearin' forest land for horses. He was always talkin' 'bout horses. "Gonna clear me out some land an' buy a buncha horses an' breed 'em, soon as'n Ah git the money," he'd say near ev'ry day it seemed.

Ain't no one b'lieved him, least not me or Ma, anyway, 'cause he talked a lot but never did. But sure enough, one day he started clearin' the land for 'em horses, a-cuttin' down trees and vines with his chainsaw, and me and my brother had to drag all that stuff to the big ditch by the road. I must'a hated that more 'an any other chore, 'cause it was all day, and we was draggin' and draggin', couldn't play or nothin', and he'd get far off ahead with that chainsaw, a-cuttin' trees a hundred times faster'an we could drag 'em, so it'd seem like we'd never finish.

Sometimes, he'd stop, and that noise from the chainsaw'd stop and ev'rythin' in the woods would fall quiet, 'cept for the poppin' of the branches we was draggin'. Real quiet, 'cause you know all the animals don't wait around when you got a chainsaw buzzin'. Well, he'd sit to drink or eat and then we'd work like crazy people tryin' to catch up with him, draggin' and dumpin', cuttin' up our hands all panickin' not knowin' when that saw'd start up again.

But it would, and we'd still be far behind. Well, anyway, after clearin' a big patch of land, he had to burn out all the underbrush, so he'd have land to plant grass for grazin' on. But somethin' went bad wrong and before we knowed it there was Ma hollerin' on the phone, draggin' us out to the car and drivin' out by the road. Pa and a bunch of other men was there in that ditch we dumped those trees. They was shovelin' dirt and such, and Lord there was a fire higher'an a house burnin' up ev'rythin'. Ma said Pa was an idiot and was yellin' all the way to Uncle Dave's while a buncha fire trucks ran screamin' past us.

Well, after all that, after the fire was out, when me and my brother went back out to the woods to play, we found a bulldozer out in the middle of the woods. That was a thing to see, let me tell you, 'cause a big yella bulldozer don't blend in with a green forest. And behind it was a big path it made, a plowed road'a dirt, and on one side'a the woods was burnt black and the other was all fine. It was to keep the fire all on one side, you see. And it sure did work.

But me and my brother, we weren't so much int'rested in that fire and all, even if it was somethin' to see as it was burnin'. That bulldozer and the road it made – well you can guess how two kids would'a liked that. That road lasted mor'an a year, even though rain and wind and all beat down on it, and it cut right by that old tire swing, which weren't burnt, so we'd play war there, the swing bein' an airplane, and that road enemy front lines.

Anyway, what I was gettin' at was that 'em bulldozers can tear up the ground like nothin' else, and so after they bulldozed the Junk Man's place, there weren't no hope of findin' nothin' at all like that heart necklace or anythin' else.

So, I just stopped lookin'. It's a shame really, 'cause I knowed for sure the story of the heart necklace. Well, that weren't my name for it. I never had no name. The Junk Man, after he saw it, called it the heart necklace.

It was right after Ma and Pa split up, and I saw Ma goin' through stuff and cleanin' up after we moved. That's when she found it. It was real pretty, all silver, but it ain't never turned black like other silver. I reckon it was a special kinda silver that don't never turn black or need polishin'. It had a silver chain with a silver heart hangin' off it. And, you know, it was a filigree heart too, like the gold Alter Ring. Pa gave it to Ma some special day, I reckon.

Well, Ma just sat there starin' at it and cryin'. I was hidin' behind a door and all, 'cause I didn't want her knowin' I seen her cry. But I did. Not just that day, neither. Lotsa times. Well, she wiped her eyes and said, "Damn him," and took the heart necklace and throwed it in the trash. I ain't never heard Ma cuss before, 'cause she's right religious and don't take to no foul mouth language, and I was real unhappy seein' all that. Well, afterwards, I snuck in and found that necklace. I hid it in my room. I don't know why. I just couldn't let her toss it out, I s'ppose.

Well, after I saw the Junk Man's museum, I knowed what I hadda do with 'at necklace. So, I took it to him and told him all 'bout it, and he lis'ened real quiet and serious, and turned the heart over in his hands again and again. His hands was real dark and dirty, and the silver was like a light in 'em. Then he said, "Well, boy, what pile you figure fo' it?"

And I said, "The special pile."

"Reckon so?"

I nodded my head, yes.

"Yeah," he said, "I reckon that ain't no hard one. I got a right good place fo' it, an' fo' the decoratin'. Sure is an awful pretty Heart Necklace. Ain't no piece of junk, right?"

"No, Sir."

"Sure ain't. You reckon any ol' person would'a thought much on it if you ain't kept it, if it come to the trash?"

"No, Sir. I reckon they'd'a thought it was some ol' piece'a junk."

"That's right, boy. But, it ain't no junk."

"No, Sir. It ain't."

So, he gave it its own place, right next to some old wood table with a bright, green peacock feather and a book. The book was wonderful nice, all leather with two belt buckles holdin' it closed. It was called "Through the Fire" and inside it was some kinda fairy tale, but a fairy tale 'bout fairies – really, I ain't kiddin'. These fairies were in love but they couldn't be together because one was a fire fairy and the other was made outta water. I reckon that's why it was with the other broke hearts, 'cause you can't put fire and water together. I never did find out what that feather meant.

"This heart necklace boy, she's gonna take her place with the other hearts broken." And he waved his long arm 'round, showin' me I s'ppose that all the tables near was filled with stories like this, like it was their own special corner of the museum.

After that day, I ain't never looked at no trash the same way. Could've been my Ma's necklace throwed out, or somethin' like it. I reckon you never can tell 'bout a thing less'n you look hard 'nuff. The Junk Man, well, he learned me that.

So, after that, knowin' I weren't never gonna find nothin' there under that river'a dirt from that bulldozer, I never went back no more. Not nowhere in the Trash Yard. And I s'ppose that really was the end of it.

9

So, now I live in a new place, far away from the Trash Yard, and got a new school. Ma split with Dan, and it's just us three – Ma, me, and my brother. I s'ppose I like it better that way. I mean, Dan was nice and all, but he weren't my Pa, and I reckon it's better havin' just a Ma than some man tryin' to be your Pa but who just ain't. That's how I feel, anyway.

Ma's always tired nowdays, workin' two jobs, and she's always snappin' at somethin'. We're hard up for money, I s'ppose. She's always writin' checks with no money and then puttin' some in the bank before the check gets there. She tells me stuff like that now 'cause she says I'm the man of the house. She's always tellin' me 'bout how she feels, 'bout stuff at her job, ev'rythin' happin' to her, what's wrong with Pa and

Dan and other men, and tellin' me not to be like all 'em men. Says she's gonna knock it outta me.

Way I'm figurin', less'n she find better work, we'll be movin' back with gra'ma again - could be this time me an' Tom'll get that basement all t'ourselves. But I'm wishin' she would go an' get better work. She ain't never got no nice stories, workin' at that jail with all 'em crim'nals and how they cut some little girl's throat or did the deed with some Thanksgivin' turkey 'cause they was on 'em drugs and whatnot. I know all the stories 'cause I guess Ma's countin' on me mor'an more.

My brother won't have nothin' of it. He don't go in much for lis'enin' to Ma's problems. He gets a look on his face, like he's mad or far'way. These days he's out with his friends nearly all the time. I hear tale he's a wild one now, 'bout gettin' himself killed and racin' on the highway and such. So, without Pa or Dan or some other man I reckon I'm 'bout all Ma has.

I mean who she got but me? She said me doin' what she needed was what kept her from a heart attack, so, would I want her dead? 'Course no – I s'ppose sometimes things can be so bad that a mom could die less'n her son helps her by bein' the man of the house.

So, a Ma might need'a ask a son for just 'bout anything. Some nights get worser'an others. Her drinkin's what makes it bad, as I'm seein' it. And she's drinkin' more and more, these days. If'n I get home and I see she's on that porch a-drinkin', I know all kinda bad things must'a happened. Most'a the time that's what it is, and I ain't got no idea how Ma works that job every dang day. I wouldn't, no Sir. There's 'bout a million other things I'd be doin' 'stead'a that. And if'n there weren't nothing else, well, I guess I'd sign up at that Army place or somethin'.

If'n they'd have me, what with my bad eyes and on account I'm awful thin and ain't no soldier type. And 'cause maybe I'm crazy, too. Like the Junk Man. I told you how I was thinkin' it might be catchin'? Yeah, well, look here. My hand on the top side. You see that funny place? Don't look right. Been itchin' me something awful. So, I itch it right back. Came on while I was workin' in the Trash Yard. But it ain't clearin' up. I'm wonderin' what it might be. Thinkin' maybe it might be some'a what made the Junk Man look like he did. That maybe, like that crazy'a his, I catched that off'a him, too. I don't know.

Anyway, I ain't never said nothin' to no one 'bout the Junk Man, I mean after it all happened. And Ma acts like it never did, so I s'ppose you're the only one's gonna hear it all, even if it's only some dumb story 'bout a crazy leper and some poor kid. Well, you lis'ened to the end, anyway. I gotta thank you for it.

You might be wonderin' why I told you all this. 'Bout the Junk Man, I mean. Well, I figured somebody just hadda hear 'bout it, not only 'cause somebody hadda know 'bout him 'cause he's gone and they did him wrong. That ain't all. What's more, if I didn't share it, it'd be like I was holdin' somethin' back from ev'ryone.

I mean, all of us, we just throwin' stuff out. Breakin' nice things and just tossin' 'em away. And that just gets me all down and wantin' to just sit and watch the boats by the dock 'til there ain't no more.

Then, the day's over and you can watch the sun hit on the water like a big ol' eye. Maybe you feel like that too, sometimes, if'n you think too much on things. I don't know.

Well, if you do, maybe you can think on what I told you, 'bout the Junk Man. 'Cause when I feel like that, I like to think on him, 'cause he'd always take what was broke and throwed out, and make it like new. Like a *new* thing.

And, you know? You can't find enough money in the whole world to buy somethin' like that.

ACKNOWLEDGMENTS

Many thanks to all the "beta-readers" out there who volunteered their time to get through what must have been for most an idiosyncratic, difficult to parse, and somewhat confounding narrative.

Special thanks to Ria Evans and KimBoo York who agreed to give their input not only on the story (in one case, inducing a radical change), but to share their personal PhDs in the Southern Vernacular as dey done larned it. Without their commentary, things would be even more absurdly clumsy than they are.

Thanks to my daughters who lifted my spirits after their reading by enthusiastically and without hesitation telling me that it was the best thing I'd written. While that of course might not be saying much, coming from the brutally honest voices of my young ladies (one who did not even finish my first thriller, at one point writing in the margin "Please, kill me now!"), it was a sorely needed vote of confidence for a book I often wondered myself what to make of.

Finally, to all the members of my family and friends who have supported my efforts to produce creative materials, who have encouraged me to "be myself" and in the words of Neil Gaiman to "make good art", this book is for you, too.

It's the closest I'll ever get to art.

ABOUT THE AUTHOR

www.erecstebbins.com

I am a biomedical researcher
in New York who writes
political and international
thrillers, as well as
undertaking excursions into
other genres. My stories
often come from the raw
emotional conflicts created
by contemporary events

around us. I strongly believe that the best stories
challenge us, so I try to create art with a certain kind of
relevant edge, at least as I experience it.

I was born in the Midwest. My mother worked as a
clinical psychologist, and my father was a professor of
romance languages at the University Nebraska in
Lincoln. In fact, his specialty, old romance languages
and their literature, is the source of the strange spelling
of my middle name: "Erec". It is an Old French
spelling, taken from an Arthurian romance by Chrétien
de Troyes written around 1170: Érec et Énide. Had my
brother been a girl, he would have been named Enide.
Instead, he's Michael.

I have pursued diverse interests over the course of my
life, including science, music, drama, and writing. My
academic path focused on science, and I received a
degree in physics from Oberlin College in 1992, and a
PhD in biochemistry from Cornell University in 1999.

OTHER BOOKS BY EREC STEBBINS

The Ragnarök Conspiracy
(2012, Seventh Street Books)

"Outrageously entertaining: epic, explosive, subversive, engaged and compassionate, like a Michael Bay movie written by Aaron Sorkin." -Chris Brookmyre, author of *Where The Bodies Are Buried*

A Western terrorist organization targets Muslims around the world, and FBI agent John Savas is drawn into a web of international intrigue. To solve the case, he must put aside the loss of his son and work with a man who symbolizes all he has come to hate. Both are drawn into a race against time to stop the plot of an American bin Laden and prevent a global catastrophe.

"Fortify your shelf of Armageddon thrillers with this promising newcomer." -Library Journal

Reader (2013, Twice Pi Press)

VICTIM: Enslaved after her parents' murder.
FREAK: Deformed, modified against her will.
MESSIAH. She opened the Orbs and begins a galactic rebellion.

Join the cosmic quest of seventeen-year-old Ambra Dawn, *Reader*, because in the end, the most unbelievable step in the adventure - will be your own.

Reader

1

The dream always began well.

It was a moist and warm spring afternoon, and a soft breeze blew over the lush grass of our backyard towards the house, carrying the strong smells of the newly tilled earth. I could not have been more than five years old, and the sun partially blinded me as I ran over the grass toward the edge of our corn fields, stumbling on my short legs, yet not falling, my arms stretched out to embrace a tall shadow in the light before me.

Suddenly, the sun was dimmed as my father's broad frame eclipsed its radiance, and the shadow transitioned instantly into his familiar form. I leapt into his outstretched arms squealing, and his soiled hands caught me tightly and swung me around as I giggled, staring into his bright blue eyes framed under locks of golden red hair. Then he tossed me upward. The ground below me, half green from grass, half rich brown from the newly plowed field, receded as the blue sky enveloped me, and I felt the thrilling tug of gravity grab my stomach, and pull me back to earth. Several times he threw me, and I went farther and laughed harder each time. Higher and higher I soared, until the blue turned black, and the Earth below became a mere sphere, dotted with continents and oceans, and above the stars shown through the thinning atmosphere.

For a moment, I floated, thrown so high I nearly escaped the bonds of gravity tying us to our home world, and the stars seemed to tug at me as well, beckoning me, luring me, with a cold intensity that my child's senses felt as vaguely threatening. My giddiness began to turn to anxiety, as I felt something wrong, something impure out there that waited in the diamond-pricked blackness in front of me. Something searching...*for me.*

But then I began to fall again, the air rushing over me, through clouds and air currents, seeing the ground first as a patchwork of squares and rectangles as from an airplane, resolving slowly to the familiar patterns of our neighborhood, and at last, that of my own family's farm. Spinning slowly in my downward trajectory, I saw my father from above, patiently waiting for me, arms outstretched with hands held high to catch me. The air whipped my clothes backwards behind me as I hurtled downwards. Wasn't I going too fast, falling without aid from the edges of space? How could he possibly slow my momentum, catch me before I plunged devastatingly like some fiery meteor into the ground?

But he did. With a slight impact, I was caught and safe in his arms, some extra momentum diverted into a swinging motion, once more spinning me in circles until I laughed. Slowly, he came to a stop, and set me on the ground, my head a mess and dizzy, my legs wobbly. He smiled down at me, tussled my hair and said, "Only you can go so high, Ambra Dawn. You were meant for more than just this place."

His words seemed so lovingly spoken, and yet in my heart echoed ominously. And, as if in answer to my deep fears, his face clouded, and he focused behind me, rising from a partial stoop and gazing across toward our house. My eyes followed him upward, and then my entire body turned to track his gaze.

Standing outside the back door that exited from our kitchen was my mother, her long red hair caught like a sideways waterfall in the

breeze. Yet she stood so still. *So terribly still.*
Her face was frozen in stone, anxiety, fear etched
in every line. One arm was raised at ninety
degrees to her body, pointing like an arrow in
front of the house. She remained pointing,
unmoving, like some directional sign indicating
the path we must follow.

My awareness sped towards her, stopping in
front of her face, then turned and followed her
arm from the bright light of the day outside and
into the dim blackness of the kitchen, through
the inside of our house, and then out again from
the front door.

Three black cars with tinted windows were
parked in front of the house. Out of these cars
stepped a troop of tall men in suits and dark
sunglasses, several of them very broad and
muscular, with earpieces and wires dangling
from them. I found myself no longer in a small
child's body, but now inhabiting that of a pre-
teen of eleven years. They brushed me away and
herded my parents into the house, and I followed
behind them feeling ignored and unwanted. A
terrible sense of foreboding hung over me, and
the darkness of the men's suits seemed deeper
than that of the space I had gazed into only
moments before.

Short, and yet long separations of time. The
way of dreams. For me, the way of life.

They sat around the kitchen table, the
smaller men talking to my parents, the larger
ones posted like soldiers around the house and

out by their cars. My mother was getting very anxious. She spoke with a shrill note in her voice. The small room was so still and quiet after the wind and openness outside.

"I don't understand. We don't know who you are. We just can't turn her over to you without more information, whatever you say."

"Ma'am," said the smallest man, with a raspy voice that made my skin crawl, "we are a special governmental division, and have developed unique technologies for the military. One of these is a special type of laser. Army doctors have shown that it can be used to kill cancer cells. We can promise you a full cure, without major side effects. No one else can. But this is top-secret technology. We cannot share this with you or anyone else – not even your doctors. Therefore, her treatment must remain secret."

He took off his dark glasses, and stared at my mom, but I was sitting behind and couldn't see his face. "A doctor in the Omaha unit is a friend of mine. He was direct with me – she won't live past next year with current treatments. We are your only hope."

I saw my mother tear up, and my father's jaw became set. "Now, you look here, Sir. You've got no cause to be speaking like that and upsetting my wife. This is all irregular. Government or not, it ain't my way to trust shadows. If what you're saying is true, we'll work with you. But I've got to know more."

"But Frank, you heard him," my mom began.

"Never you mind what he said. I don't like this talk. We ain't shopping for some used car right now."

Just then, I dropped the wooden toy I was holding in my hands. It was a small hand-carved globe, with all the continents embossed on the surface. I can see it now hitting the wooden floor with a thud and rolling out of the kitchen to the living room. My heart constricted. *The Earth! I did not want to lose it!* The man in the dark suit with his back to me turned around, and then I screamed.

I couldn't help it. I was only eleven, and it was too much for me. That demon face – I had seen it before. In another dream. Dreams within dreams. His face was part of a foggy future vision, one I had forgotten, and which rushed back through me like nails in my veins. Flashes of future memories whipped through my mind, of pain, and fear, and loneliness, and horror – all connected to this face grinning back at me like some fiend from hell.

I ran. I jumped from my seat and ran like I've never run in my life. Behind me I half-heard the shouts of my parents calling my name, and the harsh barks of this man to his soldiers. "Get her!" Then, the horrible screams of my parents behind. But I could not stop running. That terrible sense in a dream of a monster approaching from behind grew within me, and I could feel its breath and fangs approaching, gaining ground, nearing to grapple my back and legs.

I ran so hard I thought my chest would explode. Across the manicured green of our backyard, into the high fields of corn that spread out like a sea on all sides, grown thick now near harvest season. The stalks slapped me in the face, on my arms, across my chest as I ran, my breath like deep wheezings from some dying thing. Where was I going? I didn't know. *Away. I had to get away.* "On the other side of the cornfields," something screamed in my mind. There was safety, if I could just get through the fields, to the road, I would find a car, someone to take me to get help and protect me from the monsters following behind. I was close. My panting was like a windstorm in my mind. *So close.*

And then a sharp pain, a bright light like a flash in my eyes, and I was on my back, a dark figure towering over me. Warm liquid trickled down from my nose, and I felt too weak to move.

A second figure stood over me, blocking out the light of the day. In the shadow of his body, I saw that demon face again, smiling, laughing as he stared down at me.

"We've been looking for you for a long time, little girl. Don't think you can escape. Don't *ever* think you can escape from us. We have plans for you."

I couldn't respond: fear, pain, and nausea swept over me, and the world above me shrank to a small point as darkness filled in the sides. In a moment, all was black, and the sky was gone.

The same dream. Experienced countless nights. Memories of the past recreated. But this time, it did not end with the darkness.

In that absolute black, I heard voices. *Your* voices. Millions of them, rising like an ocean of sound, a chorus calling to me across the ever changing fabric of Time. And in that half-asleep state, moments before waking, when inspiration meets the practicality of day, I *knew*.

The answer was clear before my mind.

2

Nothing is ever as it seems, or is as it might be.

Stay with me for a while, hear my story, and then you'll understand. Understand just how different everything around you is from how you now believe it to be, and maybe come to terms with just how important you are to what might someday come to be.

On the cover of this book you're reading, is an author's name. He believes this story is full of his ideas, born from his own mind. It's not. *I* am writing it *through* him. In his reality, it's all part of a clever plot he's stitched together, even down to this very sentence that says he *isn't* writing it. Instead, it is the effort of my mind reaching out, back through what you call Time, and inspiring his mind, shaping his thoughts, convincing him of this reality.

Sound crazy?   Well, then, fasten your seatbelt.

I'm not exactly happy about doing this, playing puppet master with this citizen of your time. But our need is hopelessly desperate. More than you can imagine has been lost. And we are left with nothing but ashes in the cold of space.

And I've done worse. This is dangerous, both for his mind, and my own. Already, I have failed many times to send my message, and my efforts wrecked the receiving minds, driving them to madness. At other times, what has come out of the author has been a story so distorted, so warped by his own imaginings, that the message is lost, and can't achieve its purpose. Your libraries hold some of these disasters. I can only hope that this, my last effort, will not fail.

There is so much to explain, so much that you need to understand before you can accept the message, and take the step we so desperately need you to take. So many things - strange things, horrible things. Things that can't possibly be true, but are.

You'll need to understand something about Time. This may be the greatest stumbling block. Alone, it's like a monolithic stone, an arrow marching forward like some godlike unstoppable force, rolling through history. What has happened, is frozen in the Past, untouchable and unchangeable, and what will happen, the Future, is determined by the Now. But the Universe laughs at such simple ideas.

The first thing you need to let go of is the idea that Time *is* alone. *Space* and time go together, and feed off one another, in grand loops and dances that change both. I know this, because this dance plays before my mind's eye like a rainbow in the mist.

Because of this, you must let go of the idea of the Past as set, and the Future something that does not exist. *Space-time* is an ever-existing clay trapped inside the great bubble we call the Cosmos, and like clay, it can be shaped, changing past, present, and future. Always with rules. But not yet with rules any creature has come to fully understand.

Sadly, these are only abstractions, colorless phrases that teach little and distort much of the living experience. I hope that you will understand more as you hear the story.

But it is only because of these truths that I can even reach you now, and only because of them that I need to. You see, as much as the future can reach back into the past, the *past* can reach *forward* into the future. And in our time of need, we need you of our recent past. You have a part to play in righting a terrible wrong, saving billions of lives, and reversing the horrific fate that has descended upon humanity. Somehow in these pages I must convince you of this. May I be forgiven if I can't.

My parents called me Ambra Dawn, and I am a Reader. But this is *our* story.

3

I was born in the yellow-green cornfields of Nebraska.

My father was an independent farmer, one of the last not bought up by the great agribusiness corporations of the Twenty First century. When I knew him, he was a tall and lanky man in his mid-forties, of Scottish heritage, his fair skin always reddened and hardly tanned in the long summer seasons. He had crisp blue eyes and large hands that could tear open an ear of corn in a single fluid motion. When I was a small child, before I was taken from my parents, he would hold me in those huge hands like a small ear of corn, often tossing me high into the air as in my dream, and laughing until a thousand lines creased his face.

.

He had a real gift for predicting the weather. Not trained in any meteorological sciences, he was a more accurate forecaster than the U.S. Weather Service, which saved more than one harvest. It was one sign of the terrible genetics that would combine to produce me.

My mother was from a Celtic background too - an Irishwoman new to the United States. She *found* my father more than she met him, with a sense of destiny that she helped make come true. She looked like a stereotype out of a book of fables - a classic lady of the Green Isle, pale and red-headed, fiery in spirit and with her tongue. The recessive genes just keep adding up.

Even more than my father, she *forecast*, but she forecast broadly into many areas of life. Maybe four hundred years ago they would have burned her at the stake for witchcraft, but my mother was a devout Catholic, and used no spells or prayers to divine the future. Such things just came to her. As I would learn painfully, they came not from the supernatural, but from the all too natural, buried deep within her brain, in a soft spot of unusual tissue and blood vessels that any neurosurgeon, had he taken a look, would have dismissed as a small cyst – an unnatural growth of little significance.

Two years after they were married, I was born.

I got my mother's red hair, green eyes, both parents' skin that seemed to combine in me to the palest white possible outside of albinism, and, the real kicker, a combination of genes that led to a tumor right in the place my mother's small psychic cyst lay. We'll get back to that soon, because without the tumor, none of this would have happened that I am going to tell you.

In the beginning, I was just a normal farm girl. Well, maybe *normal* isn't the right word. I was *definitely* a farm girl, though. By the time I could walk, I was playing with the animals, rolling in hay, and happier out in the air with the earth under my feet than anywhere else. How cruel is the irony when I think back on what has happened to me. What I would give now to see the sky again, to feel the earth underneath, or to run through my hands the fresh soil after it was plowed. To even know it was still there, that it existed *somewhere* - that would be enough, more than I would ask for after this terrible journey.

But, normal, no, I guess I can't say I was ever really normal. Normal means seeing things and reacting to things like most people. Looking like most people. Being treated like most people. One after the other, I lost all these things.

First to go was seeing things like most people. Even early on, I think my mother knew something was different about me. When I got old enough to notice such things, it seemed that she was always looking at me like someone would an artifact from another world. She loved me, but she sensed there was something *other* about me that even a mother's love couldn't get beyond. Maybe it was her own sixth sense. But somehow, she *knew*.

In a way, that was good, because I never had to worry about surprising her or letting her down. I don't think my dad ever really knew, not even when they came to "cure" me. Which was good in its way, since his love never had any walls to get through and always reached me.

But the first time I realized I was a freak was when my dog died.

I was eight years old, and our sheepdog Matt had been with us from a few years before I was born. Getting up there in dog years. Up to that point, I had experienced many wild and strange dreams. After I told some to friends and even my parents, I learned by their reactions that some things bothered others and were best left inside my own head. Crucified unicorns, roaches crawling out of my eyes, light beams causing holes to sprout pouring blood from my arms - that kind of thing. But I had learned by then the difference between reality and dream. Or so I thought.

Then one night I dreamed that Matt died. In a thunderstorm, he was running around barking like he does at the deep subsonic roll that drives a dog crazy with sound, and in a flash of lightning, he seized up, just fell over, dead. In the dream, I could see inside him, saw the clot in his heart, watched the life like some light dim in his mind. I woke up shaking and afraid, but I didn't tell anyone. And that was the last I expected to experience of it.

Three weeks later, a storm front rolled in from the West. When relatives would visit from other parts of the country, my dad would always talk about the weather and make his flat joke (as my mom called it): "Well, it's really flat out here this time of year." Nebraska is *really* flat, and you can see the storms coming for hours in the daylight, an express train made out of dark, gray mountains pushing like a tidal wave across the planes. I started shaking again, not because I am afraid of storms, but because I was afraid of *this* storm. Because I had seen it before.

Then the sun darkened, and the rain poured down on us like syrup, and I watched like I might a horror film on TV the replay of my dog barking and running, and falling over dead in the grass. This time I couldn't see through him. But I knew. I knew what was inside.

And I knew I was a freak.

It's hard to be normal when you don't see things like other people. In my case, I saw things that no one else could see. Visions in Time. Not intuitions, not a vague sense of doom or excitement – *visions*. They began in dreams, but soon came even in the waking day. Not only visions of the future – for a Reader, it's actually a lot easier to see into the past. Visions of what was, and sometimes, what was to be, came more and more frequently, disturbing my days and my nights, pushing me further and further from people, walling me off from the normal world. Believe me, when you have seen your own birth, watched your mother scream in agony as she pushed you into the world like some deformed lump of lasagna, it changes you. When you can't tell anyone around you these things, not even your parents, you are trapped in a prison where you slowly form your own thoughts. *Different* thoughts. Thoughts that shape you inside and out.

And that is when you lose the ability to think like normal people.

By the time I was ten, I was one odd little girl. I couldn't really relate to the kids at school, or to any adults. All I had were my own thoughts, and, of course, the visions. Like some ghostly companion, they were always with me, playing reels behind my eyes, movies only I could watch. Some boring. Some interesting. Some horrible. Things I knew were somehow real, or feared would be real.

I became ostracized by my peers. My teachers couldn't reach me. My parents became very concerned. Finally, they took me in for evaluation. A few examinations by psychologists, then doctors, and, at last, neurologists. Brain scans. *Finally* there was something concrete they could hold onto, something clearly wrong with me, something to explain all the weirdness and problems.

And something that brought me to the attention of those dark forces that really control the fate of our world.

Now available: A storybook of love and loss
for not-quite grownups.

a fairy's tale

The Caterpillar
and the Stone

Erec Stebbins

Fantasy remains a human right: we make
in our measure and in our derivative mode,
because we are made: and not only made,
but made in the image and likeness of a
Maker."

—J.R.R. Tolkien, On Fairy-Stories

Available in print and as a narrated ebook.